Beweddian

Charles Barnitz

BLOOD AND THUNDER PRESS

Cover by Georgie Nelson
Cover photograph by Charles Barnitz
Author photograph by Martha Warner

BLOOD AND THUNDER PRESS

3612 Sheffield Lane
Colorado Springs, CO 80907
www.bloodandthunderpress.com

ISBN-10: 194046921X
ISBN-13: 978-1-940469-21-8

For Andrea and John, patrons of the arts

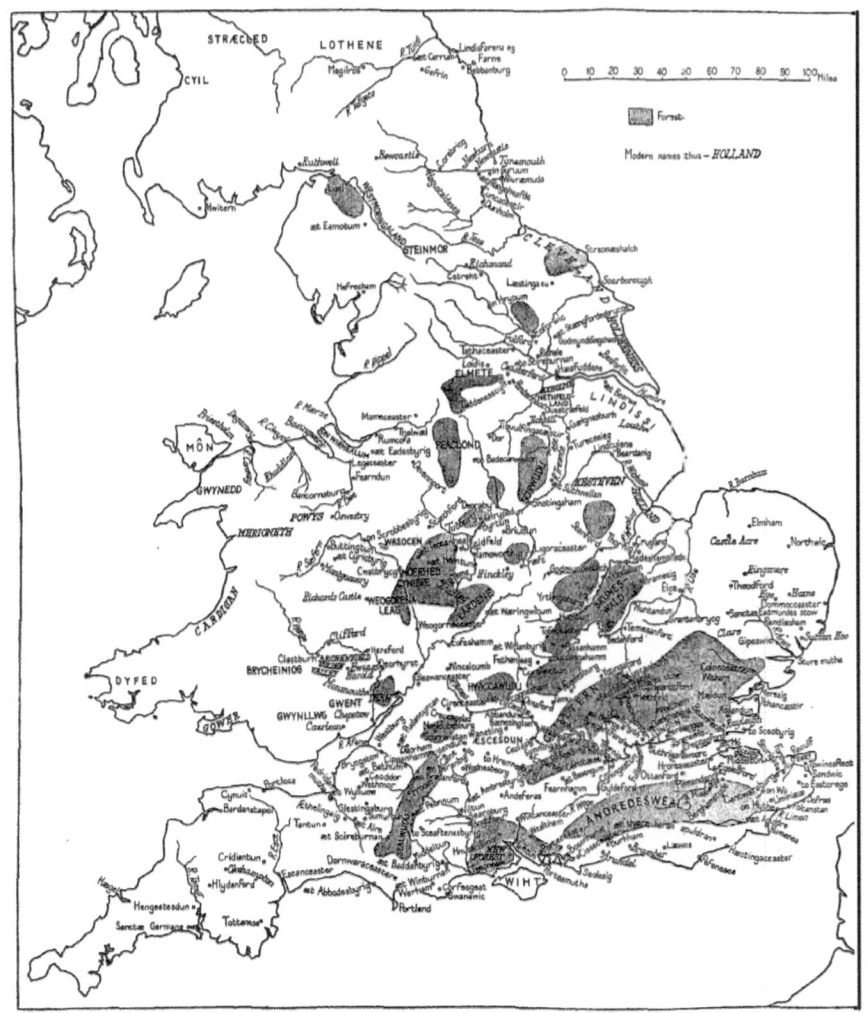

Anglo-Saxon England   Sir Frank Stenton

1

It is better to marry than to burn.

1 Corinthians 7:9

Elmet 783
(Blót-mónap)

Wulfnoth

he old *thegn* **walked** down to the barn to
see that the cattle had sufficient fodder,
checking up on the *ceorls* the way he'd
done every day of his life on the *tún*. His wife was
in the long house putting the meal together before
she and her two women, the wives of *ceorls* who
worked on the hidage, stripped off the sleeping
linen and blankets and carried them down to the
stream to wash, the way she did the first Monday
of every month, or Tuesday—sometimes the days
became slippery and elusive and it took a concentrated effort to sort them out.

He thought about his wife, her smile, her walk,

the smell of her in bed before sleep carried them away, and looked around the tún they had lived on for so many winters, finding himself standing in the middle of the open area between the barn and the house, chickens and a few geese strutting in the hard dirt, himself barefoot and chilly, wearing only a thin wool tunic and no trousers, wondering where he was going and what he'd intended to do there.

He looked toward the barn and remembered that he was going to check on the cattle fodder and make his selections for the winter cull, but he couldn't hear any cattle, and he saw that the gate to the rail enclosure beside the barn was open. "God damn it," he muttered. "Who left the focking gate open? Where are the focking cattle?"

One of the geese, a big gander, was stalking him. It paused, watching Wulfnoth stand indecisively, and then it lowered its body, thrust its neck forward, and pointed its pumpkin-colored beak aggressively at the old man, resuming its slow approach. The hissing caught Wulfnoth's attention and the old man turned to face it. The gander was a formidable, nasty-tempered, territorial bird, a good stone and a half in weight, and it bullied anyone who would put up with it — deriving particular enjoyment from terrorizing the young grandchildren, nipping at their legs and flailing at them with its wings.

The trees were mostly bare, and windblown leaves scuttled ahead of a light breeze from the west. His bare knees were cold. He could smell distant smoke. The ground was still tinged white by last night's hard frost, and when he looked back he saw where the warmth of his bare feet had melted his footprints into the white dusting all the way from the long house. He looked over the wall of the tún at the wood line that bordered the home field, confused by the conflicting cues. It looked like autumn, but the gander was acting as if it was protecting a spring nest. Was it the end of the last long winter or the beginning of the next one? The gander was persuasively territorial, so he reckoned there must be a nest somewhere that the gander was defending, which meant that spring must be coming. Then he remembered that the laying nests were in the barn where the geese stayed at night with a dog to keep the weasels and rats and stoats away. The gander had seen him walking toward the barn and it was defending its territory.

"Fock you," Wulfnoth told the gander and started toward the barn again.

The gander spread its wings and stalked rapidly toward him and when it was close enough the old man kicked out at it, sending the fowl honking and hissing away. The bird gathered itself and turned around and spread its wings again and rushed him, hopping off the ground and flapping up to shoulder height, and Wulfnoth took a step backward and thrust his left arm out to ward off the attack. The bird snapped its head down, striking him on the forearm with its chisel-pointed beak, and he punched it with his right fist, sending it squawking to the ground in a flutter of wings and honks and a small flurry of white and buff-colored down.

The gander landed awkwardly and righted itself and then circled Wulfnoth, who faced the angry bird, fists up.

"Come on, focker," he said. "You want me? I'll have you for dinner if you don't back off. Ganders are two-a-penny in the poultry market."

The gander launched at him again, beating at Wulfnoth's head with its wings but keeping beyond the reach of his fists. Wulfnoth swung and missed, and the gander's wing slapped the side of his head before it dropped to the ground and circled to the left. Wulfnoth looked around for a weapon but there was nothing handy. He knew there was a flail in the barn but the goose was keeping itself between him and the building, all angry, menacing hisses and sharp honks.

Wulfnoth reached for his seax, but his fingers closed on emptiness where the hilt ought to have been. He looked down and discovered again that he was barefoot and wearing only a tunic that reached a little below mid-thigh and that he wasn't wearing his seax. With a shout he attacked the gander, shuffling forward, waving his arms, making himself as big as he could.

The gander dodged aside and rose into the air, diving at Wulfnoth's shoulders. He felt the hard beak strike his back at the top of his spine and he spun around and hit the gander a glancing blow with his fist, deflecting its momentum. The bird landed on the ground and lowered its head again.

"You evil focker," Wulfnoth snarled. "You're going to taste good swimming in gravy with a nice chestnut and mushroom stuffing." He put his back to the barn and started sidling toward the open door to his left.

He could feel the ache where the gander had struck with its beak, all of its weight behind the blow; the skin was broken and bleeding and the impact had gone all to way to the bone; it had been like getting hit by a stone thrown at close range. He brushed his hair out of his eyes and continued toward the door, and the gander launched itself at him again. He waited until the bird was almost on him and then he stepped quickly to his right and its beak hammered the side of the barn.

Wulfnoth turned back and threw his right arm around the bird, pinning one wing to its side and grabbing its muscular neck, thick as his wrist, with his left hand. They rolled along the wall of the barn, off balance as the bird bucked convulsively in Wulfnoth's grasp, pummeling him with its free wing, kicking at him with its splayed webbed feet the size of his open hands, twisting its neck in Wulfnoth's grip to try to strike him in the face with its beak. Honks and hisses and downy feathers swirled around the old man's head like ash.

"Grandfather," a woman's voice shouted.

As he and the bird rolled against the side of the barn, he saw a woman running from the direction of the house. She looked like his wife, but she was younger and bigger, and then he lost his grip on the gander's neck and the head — the size of a big man's fist — sailed over his shoulder, brushing his ear, and he heard the beak strike the side of the barn again, and then the wall of the barn was gone and they fell through the open door onto the dirt floor inside. Wulfnoth lost his grip on the bird's neck and the gander drew its neck back for another strike.

Wulfnoth rolled to one side and the bird skittered away and turned on him again, trailing a broken wing that angled away from its body, honking in injured goose fury. A couple of broken primary flight feathers stood away from the others on the wing and the gander was hissing with pain. It extended its good wing and came at Wulfnoth in a low, shuffling attack, the tip of the broken wing dragging in the dirt. Wulfnoth rolled to one side and tried to get his feet under him to stand, but he still hadn't gotten both legs beneath him by the time the gander was close enough to strike like a snake, and he could only swing up his forearm to block it.

Off balance, the force of the strike knocked him over on his side, and the bird pressed the attack. There was a sudden darkening in the open door behind Wulfnoth, and then the big woman was inside the barn and reaching down to intercept the gander as it closed with the old man. Two strong hands darted forward and grabbed the bird's extended neck just behind its head, choking off the honking and lifting the bird off the ground. The woman swung the huge gander around in a climbing arc and then slammed it into the ground once, twice, and then around in a level circle that stopped suddenly, so the gander's momentum carried its body over her hands and the bird's neck broke with a loud snap.

The big woman dropped the dead gander and wiped her hands on her skirt. The bird twitched in the dirt, shitting out a long bile-green turd, its beak opening and closing and then opening again. The geese in the nesting boxes were squawking and honking but none of them was leaving the safety of their nests to challenge the woman that had killed the gander. The woman knelt beside Wulfnoth and brushed his long white hair out of his eyes.

"Are you hurt?"

Wulfnoth looked at the dead gander and shook his head. The woman was familiar, and now that she was beside him and he wasn't defending himself against the deranged bird, he had a moment to study her face. She didn't look like his daughter, but her face was familiar. She helped him to his feet and he stood for a moment, steadying himself, and then he gestured to the dead bird, twitching its last in the dirt.

"Pluck it and cook it for supper," he said.

"Egwyn will stuff it with chestnuts and onions and mushrooms. You can stay to eat."

Wulfnoth walked outside the barn and went to the open gate of the cattle enclosure. There was no fresh manure on the ground, no dried manure, nothing but thumb-sized turds of goose shite, no fodder in the manger, and no water in the trough.

"Where are the focking cattle?"

"You haven't had cattle for three or four winters," the big woman said.

He turned around. In the sunlight he recognized her. His granddaughter. He tried to recall her name and couldn't, but then he opened his mouth and it just came out, "Æthelwaru."

She stepped forward and put her arms around him and he returned her embrace.

"Your grandmother will be at the stream washing the linen," he said. "Tell one of the women in the house to pluck the bird. Mind they separate the down from the feathers and keep the feathers for fletching arrows."

"Grandmother isn't at the stream," Æthelwaru said.

"She isn't? Where is she?"

"Aren't you cold?" Æthelwaru asked.

He looked down at his bare feet and the movement made his back hurt just below his neck. He reached around and rubbed the spot. He must have slept all night without changing position. That often made him stiff in the morning. His left arm was bleeding and bruised.

"Let's take the gander to the house," his granddaughter said, offering her hand like she used to do when she was a little girl.

"Where's your grandmother?"

"Grandmother's gone," she said. "You remember."

Wulfnoth tried to remember where his wife had gone. If she wasn't at the stream washing the linen, then it wasn't the first Monday of the month.

"Is it market day already?" He looked around the tún and noticed that there was no activity at all. "Where is everyone?"

"On uncle Eostan's hidage helping with the winter cull," she said.

Wulfnoth thought that must be where the cattle were, driven to his brother's hidage to be culled, the meat salted and then smoked for winter consumption, and then he remembered, faster than a hummingbird, that his wife had been dead for many winters. How many? Why was he barefoot and wearing only a tunic? He looked at Æthelwaru and she started to drift out of focus, her name went first, then her identity and relationship, and then he saw that she was carrying the dead gander by its feet and its limp neck was swinging from side to side as the fist-sized head bumped along the ground.

It was all a blank, and he was cold and his back hurt where the gander had struck him. He hated that focking bird and he could taste fresh roast goose and chestnut, onion, and mushroom stuffing. His stomach rumbled.

Inside, Æthelwaru put a warm blanket around his shoulders and had him sit beside the hearth while she built up the fire, then she cleaned the wound on his arm and wrapped a witch hazel soaked bandage around the coloring bruise. There were only two women in the long house, and looking around he could see that only a quarter of the big room looked like it got any use. The rest of it was put in order, but looked vacant. There was no bedding on most of the sleeping platform, but there was a tumbled nest of blankets and an elk hide at the corner closest to the hearth. The big trestle table was bare and the benches on either side were pushed under it, out of the way. The loom frame was leaning against the wall, cobwebbed and unstrung. The house had an abandoned feeling.

One of the women carried the dead gander away to pluck its feathers outside in the kitchen. When the fire crackled up and blazed, and he could feel the warmth on his face, Æthelwaru helped him put on some warm wool trousers and then knelt in front of him and worked thick wool socks onto his feet and then his old leather shoes, his favorite pair that fit like a second skin. He lifted his feet to the hearth and offered the soles to the warmth of the fire.

"I want to get married," Æthelwaru told him.

The old man smiled. "It's good to be married."

He looked around the house as if he expected to see his wife, dead these fifteen winters, or his children, grown now and married themselves with children, then he looked back at Æthelwaru, kneeling at his feet telling him she wanted to get married.

"I need your permission," she said.

Wulfnoth knew he was the patriarch of the kindred, although he didn't always remember that he was, stuck inside his head with whatever memories he had left, and the confusion he felt when memory deserted him.

Æthelwaru's father, Eadnoth, was his oldest son; and more and more he was assuming the role of the head of the kindred. It wasn't Eadnoth's place to grant or withhold permission. Wulfnoth narrowed his eyes in anger. It was one more example of how his son was trying to slowly supplant him. If Eadnoth was against the marriage, Wulfnoth decided he was for it. He realized the girl's familiarity was because she visited him every day, cared for him, and had earned his approval for her betrothal to Mæl.

Hardly anyone else in the kindred visited the old man, uncomfortable and distressed by the work of having even the simplest conversation with him. Æthelwaru must be counting on her grandfather's reliable dislike for Eadnoth, who was slowly stealing his position as head of the kindred, one small decision and middling responsibility at a time, taking more and more for himself and leaving Wulfnoth a prisoner on his own tún, with two women and no cattle and a spiteful gander, dead now, soon to be supper, so at least there was that to look forward to.

"What does your father say?"

"He says no."

"That shite stain. Why not?"

"He says Mæl and I are too much alike. That one of us will kill the other and drag the kindreds into a feud."

Wulfnoth pulled his feet back from the fire a little. He remembered once when he was a boy how he and his friends had gone hunting in the winter and built a fire to get warm. He'd put his cold feet close to the flames and the thick leather boot soles had absorbed and retained the heat, making his feet first comfortably warm and then uncomfortably hot. When he stood up his weight pressed into the hot leather and burned his feet and he had to jump into a snow drift to quench the heat.

He'd been hunting with his friends Eogard and Baldmund and they'd gotten three big snow hares that they cooked over the fire that had burned his feet, and later Baldmund had been killed in a fight with the Mercians and Eogard had married a woman who limped after a cart wheel rolled over her foot. He always remembered her when he remembered burning his feet in the boots—they'd been laced up so tight he couldn't take the time to shed them and had to jump into the snow. Probably because of her limp. He put his feet on the floor; the soles of his shoes were warm but not hot enough to burn his feet.

"Do you want him?"

"More than anything."

"Does he want you?"

"More than anything."

"Do you miss him when you look around and remember he's gone?"

"It's an ache in my heart."

Wulfnoth pulled the blanket a little tighter around his shoulders and leaned toward his granddaughter and kissed her on the forehead. He could smell the smoke of the fire in her hair and when he leaned back he saw that she was crying quietly.

"That shite stain," he said again. "I'll see to it."

Eadnoth **watched his father** and his daughter ride up the sloping valley toward the *tún*. Æthelwaru was late coming home. She went to visit Wulfnoth every morning, and she was usually home by midday, but now that he saw his father was riding with her, he put her lateness down to the old man. Eadnoth hadn't seen his father since the Midsummer feast, and he didn't miss him a bit. His father was in his dotage. Sometimes he couldn't remember who Eadnoth was, or claimed not to, and he was given to childish tantrums about misperceived slights and imagined insults. He lost things, misplaced items of routine use and blamed *ceorls* he distrusted because of something they'd done or not done winters before Eadnoth had been born, without realizing that the *ceorls* were dead or long gone from the hidage.

But he still looked like his old self on horseback, dressed and cloaked and booted and wearing his seax — every mounted inch of him looking like the head of the kindred and the warrior that he'd been for most of his winters, until his wife dropped dead and he went into a deep inconsolable grief. When he came out on the other side, he started to slip back in time to before his wife died, drifting, first overlooking the small things, and then the larger things, until his lapses, artfully covered by everyone's assumption that he was slow to recover from his wife's death, lingered longer than any reasonable period of mourning could explain, and he couldn't cover them any anymore.

When Eadnoth reluctantly stepped up to assume the slack and prepare himself to lead the kindred, his father accused him of trying to steal his position. It was winters more before anyone outside the kindred could see it. Men who only saw Wulfnoth at the hundred gemót or the Yule feast or in Loidis at the witangemót saw him as they'd always seen him without realizing that they were only seeing the misleading husk of what he'd been before, the same husk that was riding up the sloping home field toward the tún. By now, everyone in the kindred knew that Wulfnoth was slipping into a second childhood, and that he refused to relinquish control or to prepare his oldest son to lead the kindred when he was finally gone.

But still, this deep into his winters and his dream world, Wulfnoth was able sometimes to pull himself together and look like he was still in firm command of his mind and his kindred.

Æthelwaru rode a little behind Wulfnoth. Eadnoth could hear her talking, but he couldn't make out her words.

Eadnoth began to get a bad feeling about this visit. Usually his father kept to his own tún and Eadnoth got on with the decisions and actions that the patriarch of the kindred had to take and do without interference. It was as if his father had forgotten the details of running the kindred and the responsibilities of being the patriarch, or couldn't be bothered to make the effort, content to remain in the smaller and smaller world inside his head. Their kindred was small compared to some others, and their hidage was correspondingly modest, but there were still decisions to make, disagreements to arbitrate, and those tasks fell to Eadnoth, whether he was thanked for them or not.

His father and his daughter rode through the gate to the tún and passed him with no more acknowledgement than if he were a post. He had to follow them on foot as they rode to the stable and dismounted. He saw that his father's left arm was bandaged and Eadnoth assumed it was from one of the accidents he was more and more prone to have as the winters passed. Æthelwaru's brother, Wilnoth, came out of the stable and took the reins from his grandfather's hand and led his horse inside, leaving his sister to follow, leading her mare.

Wulfnoth looked around and spotted a fat man making his slow way toward the stable, his cloak swaying around his calves as he walked. The fat man looked familiar. He reminded Wulfnoth of his wife's uncles—all fat men, all dead. He stretched. He could hear geese honking somewhere on the tún and he felt vaguely uneasy. His arm throbbed. The fat man stopped in front of him and said, "Hello father. What brings you here?"

"The girl wants to marry," he said, coming right out with it.

Aethelwaru was walking out of the stable toward them.

"You've been whinging to your grandfather." Eadnoth said.

Wulfnoth interrupted, "Where are your brothers?"

Eadnoth looked at his father. "On their hidages." His unpredictable tangents were still surprising.

"Send for them."

"Why?"

Wulfnoth took a step toward the man who was apparently his fat son and grabbed the front of his cloak. "Because I told you to." He shook his fat son and released him.

Eadnoth shot his daughter a poisonous look and called to Wilnoth in the stable. "Ride to your uncles túns and tell them their father wants them here."

"More like it you shite stain," the old man said, starting toward the house. "Beer."

Æthelwaru followed her grandfather, leaving Eadnoth standing in front of the stable watching them walk away. "When is that focking goose going to be ready to eat?" Wulfnoth shouted.

Inside the house, Eadnoth's wife Egwyn hurried to make her husband's father welcome and comfortable, knowing that both were impossible. She pulled a chair next to the fire and brought him a cup of beer and some bread and cheese. Æthelwaru pulled a stool up beside her grandfather's chair and took the wooden plate with the block of cheese and the end of a fresh loaf from her mother and sat it on the hearth stones while Wulfnoth drank the beer in slow gulps. She took out her knife and sliced a thick slab of cheese from the block and then sliced the bread and gave them to her grandfather.

Wulfnoth took the bread and cheese from the big woman, who was attentive and sad. He'd seen the change creep over her when they rode onto the fat man's hidage and he could feel her tension now that they were inside the house.

"What's the matter girl?"

"You've got to remember your promise. You've got to remember that you're the head of the kindred and you decide whether I can marry."

"Who said I'm not the head of the kindred?"

Wulfnoth looked around the house, but there were no men there to challenge him, just women busy around the hearth and weaving on a couple of angled looms ten or fifteen feet away.

"How are your children?" he asked Æthelwaru.

"I don't have children," she said. "Father won't let me marry."

"You should have children. They're a comfort when you're old."

A rectangle of daylight opened and closed at the other end of the long room and Eadnoth emerged from the blinding contrast, walking slowly down the center of the room toward the hearth fire.

"They'll be here in a while," Eadnoth told his father. "Why do you want to see them?"

"I have something to tell you all."

The fleeting hope that his father was going to retire as the head of the kindred and formally promote him to take his place came and went so fast that Eadnoth was barely aware of its transit. It was something else, he was certain, whatever unknown thing he'd begun to dread when he saw his crazy father and his disrespectful daughter riding together toward the gate of the tún.

"Your mother said she wants to have the Yule

feast for the whole kindred this year."

"Mother's been dead for ten winters. Your youngest granddaughter doesn't even remember what she looked like."

Wulfnoth took a sip of beer, his eyes narrowing at his son over the rim of the cup. "Just for that insolence you're not invited," he said.

"Are the servants doing their job over there?" Eadnoth looked at his daughter but he was jerking his head toward the wall, in the direction of his father's tún.

"Do you care?" Æthelwaru asked.

"I've had all the sass I want from you," he said.

Wulfnoth drew his seax and laid the width of the blade on his left palm. The light sheen of oil brought up the whirling pattern in the polished surface as he turned it slowly, following the ghost reflection with his eyes.

"My father gave me this seax when I was fifteen winters old," he said. "The souls of every man I ever killed with it are trapped in the iron. You can see them when the light's just right."

Eadnoth turned away and walked outside to wait for his brothers.

Wulfnoth thought about his father's face when he gave him his seax at the midsummer gemót. He still felt like he was fifteen winters old, thought like he'd thought then, liked and disliked the same things — he wondered how he'd gotten so old and when it had happened. He wanted to remember to tell his wife about this thought, to ask her if it was the same for her, the passage of the winters, the sudden memory of something that had happened winters before that was more than a memory, more like inhabiting a memory for an instant, a spark of re-experience that came to him and began to fade as soon as he was aware of it.

The big woman touched the spotted back of his hand that gripped the hilt of the seax and whispered, "Grandfather."

He looked up. It was his granddaughter Æthelwaru, focking hell she was a big girl, taller than he was, and wide-shouldered with that big tangle of brown curls all down her back.

"Your sons are here."

He looked up and saw his five sons standing around the hearth.

"Well, what do you want?"

They looked at one another and shuffled in place. They were all big but none of them as fat as Eadnoth. The youngest but one was Eghart, and he'd been his mother's favorite. Wulfnoth had liked his second son best — Eadmer was a boy you could trust. He'd never try to steal the leadership of the kindred, not like that shite stain Eadnoth.

"You sent for us," Eadmer said.

"Who's the head of the kindred?"

"Don't you know?" Eadnoth asked gruffly.

"I know," Wulfnoth said. "I want to be sure you do."

"You're the head of the kindred, father," one of the other sons said; Wulfnoth couldn't remember his name. He wasn't sure that he'd ever seen him before, and he wondered if he wasn't one of Eadnoth's cronies, slipped in to make up the right number of bodies, thinking he wouldn't notice.

"Too focking right," he said. "And who agrees to a betrothal?"

Eadnoth cut a look at his daughter, but Æthelwaru was looking at her grandfather, still holding his hand, and she wouldn't look at him.

"That willful bitch will bring us all to ruin," Eadnoth said. "The marriage is unsuitable and dangerous. Torhtmund's son is a disrespectful idiot."

"Torhtmund? You mean Torhtmund son of Bryhtmund?"

"What of it?"

Wulfnoth remembered a young man called Torhtmund, who'd gotten his iron at the same midsummer gemót all those winters ago. Torhtmund's father was dead and his mother was dead and the stepmother — something about the stepmother — something bad — whatever it was. Torhtmund was taking his brothers and sisters and building his own tún, leaving the stepmother alone with her children. It must have been very bad for him to take his dependent brothers and sisters away from the home they'd all grown up on and establish his own tún at the age of fifteen. Wulfnoth remembered how impressed all the other boys had been, and how it made Torhtmund seem winters beyond them, but showed them, at the same time, what was possible.

"This is Torhtmund whose son's an advocate?"

"It's not the advocate we're talking about. She wants to marry the miller."

"Big lad, plain spoken?"

"That's the one." Eadmer said.

"Short tempered, stupid, and nasty's more like it," Eadnoth insisted.

Wulfnoth turned to his granddaughter. "And you want to marry him?"

Aethelwaru nodded.

"He'll give you good big sons," Wulfnoth said. "So be it."

"No," Eadnoth shouted. "It's a danger to the kindred."

"Has he made a pledge and a gift?"

"Yes grandfather," she answered.

"I accept the hand-fæstung. Now set the date."

"I won't allow it."

Wulfnoth stood up, not remembering that he was still holding his seax. "Won't allow it, you fat slug? Won't allow the head of the kindred to accept a betrothal to the son of a man he grew up with? Who are you to say you won't allow it?"

Wulfnoth's sons took a step back, the three he remembered and the two that didn't look familiar to him. He was taking his cue from Æthelwaru, and so long as she accepted that the men were her uncles, he wouldn't make an issue of it. He looked down and noticed that he was holding his seax and slipped it back into the sheath.

"Is there anything else?"

His sons looked at one another but they didn't say anything.

"Then where's that focking goose?" Wulfnoth shouted. "I'm hungry."

His sons had no idea what he was talking about.

Elmet 784
(Mædmónaþ)
Þring

It was good to be in Elmet again. The light was clearer and the sky was bluer and the air was sweeter and the road was less stony underfoot as soon as I splashed out of the Deane river ford and into the Barnsleydale hundred. I sat back in the saddle and my horse stopped as I turned my face up to the sky and breathed in the air of my home country. I fancied at that moment that I began to relax for the first time in a year. Of course, this was all a simmering waggonload of malodorous shite, because the rain that was falling on my face out of the milky, swollen clouds was no warmer or softer on one side of the river than the other, and certainly no drier. Still, it was Elmet rain, and I suppose that was something.

For the last year Banta had been dragging my

ass around Wessex, Sussex, and Cant while he taught me the tradecraft of the *sundornotu-geréfa* — the spy and killing *thegn*. Our cover was catching rats, an occupation that justified our mobility and gave us access to the venues we most desired to inspect. We had a dozen ferrets and a couple of small, vicious dogs that did most of the work, but I had to know how to do the job, so half of my training had concentrated on the techniques and tools of killing rats. Rats are everywhere, and a couple of men with trained ferrets and bad-tempered terriers are cordially welcome in every *feorm* barn, granary, grange, threshing floor, scriptorium, and monastery that can afford their asking price.

We spent the autumn wandering the country of Wessex from Oxenaforda to Escanceaster, almost never sleeping rough because there are a lot of monasteries and abbeys in the kingdom of the West Saxons. They're a devout people. They were also a restive people in the autumn of 783 — heavily armed and intent on declining the honor of being absorbed into Greater Mercia — so Cynewulf's mounted *gesithmen* and *fyrd* troops were marching on the roads from here to there, interrupting the ebb and flow of honest commerce with aggressive displays of heavily-armed, shield-banging nationalism. We made our services and our ferrets and dogs available to cellarers and sacristans and *tún-geréfas,* and in return we were given the free run of every monastery, abbey, cathedral, and royal *ville* we came to. Pretty much everything a spy can hope for. We had to clean up after the dogs, though, and as the junior man it fell to me.

We wintered in Escanceaster, the old Roman town on the River Esce at the southeastern end of the great stone road that runs diagonally across the southern kingdoms all the way to Lindesege. There was nothing unusual to discover in the monastic archives of Escanceaster, only copies of charters and wills and notes from meetings and blotted copies of boring correspondence, but, despite the absence of any documentation of interest to me, Banta believed that there were many things to be learned from the patterns of land acquisition and grants, the quantity and quality of the bequests in rich men's wills, and how much productive hidage the church gained in bequests and profession gifts, removing it from the pool of land that contributed to the three necessities.

When the weather broke in the early spring, we worked our way east at a leisurely pace, stopping at the larger towns — the old capital of Dornwaraceaster, the port and industrial market town of Hamwic, and the minster at Wimborne (582 rats *in totum*). After diverting to Wintancaester, where we'd hoped to observe the king (unfortunately he was out of town, making a leisurely progress around the kingdom), we turned south and crossed the border into Sussex and then continued east along the coast.

The South Saxons had been less successful than the West Saxons at resisting Offa's gracious offer of inclusion into greater Mercia; if you ask me, it was because of their confusion of kings (Oswald, Osmund, Ælfwald, and Oslac all ruling in rotation — or possibly simultaneously, who knows?), and Offa had taken advantage of the situation to annex Sussex about a dozen years ago. Sussex was now a Mercian sub-kingdom. This means that these days Ealdwulf isn't issuing his own charters as a *Rex* — he's making his humiliated mark on Offa's charters as a *dux* or a *sub-regulus*. We spent a week in Cisseceastre, where we got a distant look at Ealdwulf swanning around in regal style like he wasn't Offa's butt boy, and we crept through the royal scriptorium, taking our time over three nights (72 rats); then we diverted south to Sedesig Abbey and cathedral.

Wherever that bastard Wilfrið settled a cathedral sprang up like a mushroom in a pasture pie. Wilfrið had founded Sedesig Abbey after king Ecgfrith threw him out of Northumbria for assuring his young queen Æthelthryth that she didn't have to break her vow of perpetual virginity because of that inconvenient political marriage, after which assurance she'd stubbornly insisted on keeping her virginal knees together despite her royal husband's protests. Easy to see how that ended in exile for the great Wilfrið, champion orator of Streanshalch, founder of monasteries, stiff-necked bishop, and general whinging pain in the arse. He got off light if you ask me; I'd have spiked his head over the gate.

During his wandering exile, on his way back from Rome where he'd bitched long and hard to the Pope about his shitty treatment at home, Wilfrið had washed up on the Sussex shore — this was before the South Saxons had all converted to Christianity — and barely escaped the kind of unpleasant death the South Saxons specialize in.

Fifteen winters later, with a voluminous history of acrimony between himself and the majority of the bishops in Britain, including the Archbishop of Cantwarabyrig, the Northumbrian king exiled him again and Wilfrið returned to Sussex.

On Wilfrið's first visit only the king and queen of the South Saxons and their court had been Christians. In the intervening winters, only a few more of the South Saxons had converted, most hung on to the worship of gods who had proven themselves serviceable over the long haul. On Wilfrið's second visit, King Æthelwealh gave him 87 hides to found a monastery as a base of operations from which to convert the rest of the population to Christianity. This was another reason to wonder about Æthelwealh's sanity. He couldn't have been ignorant of Wilfrið's reputation as an arrogant, cock-blocking prelate and all around asshat, yet he granted him 87 hides of land together with the villages and men that lived in them, including a couple hundred slaves to do the grunt work.

Aside from the spiritual satisfaction of having

a shite in a latrine that Wilfrið might have buffed with his own saintly behind, there was nothing to discover in the archives of Sedesig Abbey but more charters and wills and the records of the *port-geréfa*, but the abbey was close to the sea and their rats were bigger and meaner and more wide-ly-travelled than inland rats, and so the monks welcomed us with the subdued hospitality usually reserved for representatives of the lower classes who can be useful.

We laid over at Sedesig for the Eastertide cele-brations and liturgical ceremonies, exterminated vermin in the cathedral foundations and crypt (86 rats, 23 mice) and then we took the direct route to Cantwarabyrig, an arduous trudge through the *Andrade Weald*, the heavily-forested ridge that sep-arates the rolling hills of the North Downs from the rolling hills of the South Downs. It was so rank and deep and buggy that I couldn't understand why the South Saxons wanted to claim it for their home let alone why anyone would want to take it away from them. It was reputed to be the haunt of dragons, but we kept well to the south of where they'd last been reported.

The *Andrade Weald* is a hundred and twenty miles wide and fifty miles deep, and its sole vir-tue, so far as I could see, is that it divides the Jutes of Cant from the Jutes of Wiht and kept them from forming a single kingdom of fractious and trou-blesome Jutes that would make real misery for everyone.

We mostly slept rough and often wet on our trip through *Andrade Weald*. If we'd pushed hard it would have taken us only a week, but Banta diverted to every little *croft* and *ham* and *tún* we passed, taking time to exterminate *feorm* barns and grain silos and halls, and even pig sties (234 rats *in totum*), making friends and contacts. Half the time we worked *gratis*, and the happy beneficiary of Banta's apparent generosity paid us in information without realizing that was the currency we preferred. At least while we were in the *Andrade Weald* the dogs could shite where they wanted. The pigs cleaned up after them.

After what seemed like a long biblical penance of bug bites and random encounters with pink-eyed, diarrhetic swineherds, we broke out of *Andrade Weald* onto the North Downs two weeks to the day after we'd first entered the forest. It took us two more days to reach Cantwarabyrig.

At the end of our third day in the city, Banta returned from a dead drop south of Cantwarabyrig in a foul mood and handed me a sealed parchment with my name written on it in runes:

ᚾᚱᛁᛏᚷ

The message contained the startling information that my brother Mæl had finally settled on a date for his wedding ceremony. After a quick read, I told Banta I was leaving for Elmet and that I'd meet him back in Tamoworthig for the midsummer feast. Even though I'd been with him for twelve months, I could see he thought I should be asking for permission, but I'd had enough of ratcatching, and I needed a respite from Banta's gritty tutelage. I was sick of those nasty focking terriers, too.

Lullo

Lullo was sitting in the household chapel where it was cool and shady and he was unlikely to be disturbed because no one in his kindred was devout or spiritual enough to visit the chapel unless they were under some liturgical obligation. He raised a ceramic bottle of mead to his lips and took a long slow sip of the cool honey liqueur. Lullo kept several bottles of mead in the locked cabinet where he also kept the sacramental wine, the chrism, and the incense. Lullo also had four bottles of mead chilling in the spring behind his house and two more in a hollow log near his mother's home field. The stone chapel was in the shade of a grove of tall lime trees that kept the interior cool on the warmest days, and the mead was always the perfect temperature on the tongue.

As the tithing priest and the mæsse-thegn of his kindred, Lullo had come to an arrangement with several of his parishioners, and they supplied him with mead and beer and cider in exchange for a schedule of lenient penances. Lullo's penitential, a pricy book that had been commissioned especially for him in the scriptorium in Cantwarabyrig to commemorate his ordination, was defaced by scrawled notes in the bastard Latin he'd learnt at Monkwearmouth to remind him of the penitential discounts he'd negotiated in return for liquid consideration. Not even Lullo's Latin teacher would have been able to decipher his penitential, which meant that his arrangements were impenetrable to his illiterate kindred, should they happen to glance at its pages, and would only enhance his reputation as a deep thinker. In fact the only thing deep about Lullo was the depth of his inebriation this early in the morning.

Monkwearmouth is one half of Benedict Biscop's double foundation where the great Bede himself trained (although Bede trained at Jarrow, the other half). But in the minds of Derehild's side of the kindred he'd trained at Bede's foundation. They seemed to think that sleeping in the same dorter and eating in the same refectory and praying in the same church and studying in the same classroom where Bede had done those things elevated Lullo's meager scholastic accomplishments, however, Lullo was one of those men whose mere presence depressed and devalued the worth of any venue in which he appeared.

After twelve years at the school at Monkwearmouth Lullo had only managed to memorize the ordinary of the mass and some random Latin phrases. His greatest linguistic achievement was mastering the sign language that allowed him to keep his belly full in the refectory where they ate in silence while they listened to edifying verses read aloud, often in Latin that was incomprehensible to him. He'd never mastered the rules of grammar and syntax that gave the five declensions of Latin nouns and four conjugations of Latin verbs their structure and meaning. All that remained of the lessons that had occupied three hours each day was a residue of random words, like flotsam clinging half way up the wall of a house after a flooded river recedes, and the phrases that were stranded in his word hoard often had little connection to one another, or to his native Anglian dialect.

What had kept Lullo in Monkwearmouth all those winters had not been his scholarship but his grandmother Derehild's steady subsidy of silver, and the generous profession gift of five hides of oak forest that, smartly managed, provided a steady revenue stream that abbot Cuthberht was loath to interrupt because of Lullo's deficient intellectual abilities.

Lullo burped, took another long swallow of cool mead, and inhaled the sweet honeyed fumes. They seemed to gather and roil in some cavity behind his eyes, and his face flushed and his eyes watered just a little as he opened his mouth and inhaled, siphoning off the fumes from the mead that he held on his tongue. He was close to the bottom of the second bottle and it wasn't yet midday. He'd told his mother, Uda, that he was going into Loidis in the afternoon to buy some incense, but that had been a misdirection that would allow him to remain in the cool, comfortable shadows of the chapel and finish three bottles of mead. Tomorrow there were confessions, and he had every expectation that one of his penitents would be restocking the cabinet in return for a marked-down penitential consideration.

He had plenty of incense, but he was short on privacy, and privacy was what he required so he could drink and brood on his miserable life as the unwilling minister to the spiritual needs of his ungrateful kindred. Lullo had hated every hour of the ten winters he'd been a mæsse-thegn just as much as he'd hated every hour of his involuntary imprisonment at Monkwearmouth, where he was supposed to be learning the craft of holiness. He detested the whining tone of the men and women he confessed and the venial scope of even their mortal sins. He despised the mysterious routine of the liturgy, whose words he understood only in half-forgotten fragments. He loathed the hypocrisy of his grandmother who made a show of her pride in his ordination but in fact had banished him to Monkwearmouth as an oblate because her stepson Torhtmund had given his son Hring to the church in Eoforwic in oblation for surviving the terrible blizzards of the previous winter.

Lullo had seen for himself at Monkwearmouth just how the bureaucracy of the Church worked; he was a drunk, not an idiot, and the scales had dropped from his eyes. He knew why the abbot kept him there, and it had nothing to do with the vocation they both knew he didn't have. His kindred, though, browbeaten by mæsse-thegns their whole lives and force-fed a diet of guilt for the unoriginal sins they committed and the Original Sin they hadn't — and their terror of divine punishment for both — were easily cowed, even so far as accepting a manifestly unworthy and reluctant mæsse-thegn like him. Lullo soon came to think of them as deluded and gullible simpletons.

It was all Hring's fault. The seething enmity between his grandmother Derehild and her stepchildren — Torhtmund in particular — made her seek out even the slightest opportunity to surpass them, and so when Hring had been expelled from the minster and returned to the kindred, his grandmother had insisted that the kindred shun Hring as an apostate. When that failed, Lullo's doom was sanctified and sealed. There was no way to escape the life he hated after that, and, as a strict adherent to the Roman tradition, he couldn't even marry to relieve the isolated tedium of his life with a woman and children.

So Lullo drank his way from day to day, irritated when called upon to perform his routine duties as a mæsse-thegn and imposed upon even to say his ordinary prayers, in Latin or in Anglian.

Lullo closed his eyes and had another long sip of mead — warm on his tongue, mellow and sweet with just a hint of the clover and honeysuckle the bees had visited. He allowed himself to think lustful thoughts about the daughter of one of his uncle Whitgar's ploughmen. She came to him for confession and, honest in the simpleminded way of devout girls, confided her unworthy thoughts and amorous urges to him in search of absolution. Lullo longed to absolve her in a way that she'd never forget, and yet he knew if he did, and were discovered, his grandmother's wrath would be terrible and endless and worse than God's wrath on judgment day.

He was thinking about what the girl would look like naked in the moonlight in a field of clover and honeysuckle still warm from the afternoon sun and his right hand was sliding toward his stiffening cock, when the chapel door squeaked open.

"Lullo?"

It was his mother, Uda. He corked the mead bottle and set it back in the cabinet before he stood up and stepped into view.

"What is it mother?"

"It's good I caught you before you left," she said. "Your grandmother wants to see you.

Derehild

erehild sat on her chair in the hall and watched her grand-daughters work at the three looms angled against the rough plastered wall, like a caricature of the pagan fates. It seemed as if she spent most of her time watching her granddaughters at the looms, and even though they weren't very good weavers, the more she corrected them, the worse their work became, so she'd learned to hold her tongue. Instead of paying attention to the details of the work, the girls preferred instead to rehash endlessly the dull gossip of their constricted lives. If her hands weren't gnarled and useless she could show them what good weaving was, but those days were gone for her. She looked at the walls where her loomwork and embroidery hung and remembered the making of every piece. Years ago.

The door opened and her grandson Lullo came into the hall. Before he'd walked three steps, she'd gauged his state of sobriety and found it wanting. He hesitated while his eyes accustomed to the dim light in the hall, and she watched him look around, and then turn his eyes in the direction he knew her chair was, not seeing her yet. What a disappointment Lullo had turned out to be, one of many in a long life, proving to Derehild that her plans and intentions were at the mercy of a whimsical fate.

It had begun, she often thought, with her decision to marry Bryhtmund all those years ago. Bryhtmund was handsome and well-established and potent, but he came with a pack of brats littered by his sainted first wife, Ældgyth, who Derehild had heard about every day of her married life, how she did this or that differently, what she liked and disliked, how she arranged the spices and the cooking utensils just so, until Derehild was so sick of her name she would have eaten live coals to keep from ever having to hear it again. And Derehild's children always lesser than Ældgyth's children, not so bright, not so strong, not so well favored. When Bryhtmund died she was relieved to be rid of the constant reminders of Ældgyth's superiority, and she began to dream of the days when she would be rid of her nasty brood of vermin.

But that was all water through the millhouse.

Torhtmund's son Hring had been an oblate and was disgraced. He'd returned to Elmet and (through Torhtmund's connections) risen in the judiciary until now, if the rumors were true, he was about to become an advocate, with all the attendant honor and respect that went with the position. Her grandson had been an oblate, taken vows, been ordained, and returned as a mæsse-thegn and no one liked or respected him. He was a drunk and a disappointment and a poor priest, despite having accomplished the task she had set him to.

Lullo began to walk toward her, the careful walk of a man who was more than marginally drunk attempting to conceal his level of impairment. Given his practice at the consumption of spirituous liquids, Derehild knew approximately how deep in his cups Lullo must be to find it necessary to concentrate on the difficulty of walking into a room. Her granddaughters saw him coming and stopped talking as they worked. There was no sound but the padded jolt of the weaving sword packing the weft and the clacking of the heavy loom weights suspended at the end of the warp threads.

"Grandmother," Lullo said. "It's good to see you."

"We've received an invitation to that oaf Mæl's wedding," she said, choosing to regard the first lie out of Lullo's mouth as one of the hundred harmless lies of deferential courtesy she was told every day. "It will happen in three weeks."

"Am I to officiate?" It was difficult to believe such an opportunity would come his way.

"They have their own officiant," she said. "The

advocate Sentwine's masse-thegn."

Lullo seemed to relax. Ever since he'd gone to Hring's tún to perform the last rites for his wife and made some poorly-remembered and intemperate remark that triggered Hring's grief-fueled rage (Derehild had no doubts, despite Lullo's denials, that Hring's version of the event was true), Lullo had been avoiding the other half of his kindred, and with good reason. But if he were present at the wedding by invitation, he was in no danger—the rules of hospitality would protect him. To break frith would be ruinously actionable at the gemót.

Whatever Lullo had said, his resulting beating by Hring had made it impossible for him to minister to Torhtmund's half of the kindred as a mæssethegn. That meant that his irritating presence, demonstrably successful in a religious capacity where Hring had so blatantly failed, was removed like a splinter drawn from a toe. Torhtmund claimed not to care that his son was expelled from the minster, or that Derehild's grandson was ordained, but Derehild knew her stepson's character and the urgency of his bone-deep drive to succeed, so she knew that every reminder of his son's failure in Eoforwic and her grandson's success at Monkwearmouth, was a needle in his spleen.

Lullo's behavior had given Torhtmund an opportunity to remove that needle, and the fact that he'd suffered for it meant nothing to Derehild, who saw the invitation to Mæl's wedding as an

opportunity to prick her stepson and his household with it one last time. Lullo was scarred exter-
nally — his nose broken, his ear torn — and internal-
ly — the beating had driven him deeper into himself, and whatever he found there made him drink
even more — but Derehild didn't care.

She said, "I want you to prepare a toast for the
wedding."

Lullo inhaled sharply and looked at her. There
was a laugh from the loom and she glanced over
to see her granddaughters sharing a smirk at their
cousin's bleary discomfort. She gave them a long
look brimming with venomous promise, and they
jerked their heads back to their work. She'd settle
with those snide little bitches when Lullo was
gone. He deserved their respect as a mæsse-thegn.
Possibly she'd suggest some harsh penances for
their next confessions. Lullo was a spiteful shite
and he'd be happy to exact a small bit of revenge if
he thought they'd been mocking him. This sort of
penitential justice was a tool that was now denied
her for Torhtmund's side of the kindred. Lullo
was to blame for that as well.

"There will be many toasts — "

"And yours will be foremost among them,"
Derehild said, cutting him off.

Lullo took that to mean that this toast she was
ordering him to deliver would be the official toast
from their side of the kindred.

"Shouldn't Whitgar give the toast?" he asked.
His uncle Whitgar was Derehild's son and the le-

44

gal head of their branch of the kindred, responsible for all their surety.

"If I know Whitgar, he'll be wallowing drunk on the floor in the bearskin, sucking up to Torhtmund's household. When it comes time for the toast he'll be in no shape to deliver it; anyway, it's for me to say who gives the toast. I say it will be you. They insulted us by not asking you to conduct the wedding ceremony, but we'll have our opportunity to speak."

Lullo realized that he was sobering up. The quiet day of drinking and feeling sorry for himself that he'd been looking forward to when he woke up that morning was now ruined, and the shadow of this conversation would hang over every day until the wedding.

"You've three weeks to compose the toast. St. Paul has much to say on the subject of marriage, as I recall."

Lullo nodded, backing away from Derehild and not turning until he was out of reach. It was an unconscious behavior that lingered from a time when he was six winters old and Derehild had called him before her chair for correction. When he turned away after an acid tongue lashing, during which he'd not seemed appropriately contrite, she'd leaned forward and clapped him soundly on the ear, which had bled and then rang and hummed like a tolled bronze bell for a month after.

Dring

t had been a hard, unsatisfying year. Coerced by the Mercians into leaving my home and my work as an advocate just when I'd returned to them, I'd spent months tramping from place to place beside a cart pulled by a spavined horse that couldn't walk as fast as I could, even though the cart was small and the load was light—a tent, cooking gear, supplies, and the caged ferrets and dogs and equipment we needed for them. When I complained to Banta that he ought to at least get a sound horse, or better yet, a mule, he reminded me that we were cultivating a cover as ratcatchers, not prince bishops on splendid processional round the diocese, and that a ratcatcher who could afford to keep even a spavined horse and a dozen ferrets and a pack of nasty, yippy little dogs was rich by ratcatching standards and already attracting enough attention.

I was used to riding the *gemót* circuit as an assistant advocate, not walking the ratting circuit as an assistant ratcatcher, and it took me a while to get into better pedestrian shape, during which time I endured constant ridicule and snide mockery until the blisters that sent me limping footsore to my blankets every night burst and dried up and hardened into calluses.

"You've a week's ride to Elmet," Banta said.

"Longer if the weather turns bad." Late spring rains are a traveler's bane.

"Take one of the ferrets. Start using what you've learned. You won't always be working with me."

"How am I to get there in a week if I'm packing a cage and tools?"

"Just take nets and a travel sack. Pick whichever ferret you like."

So that's how I came to have the ferret and a sack of hemp netting with me when I went home for Mæl's wedding. Ferrets sleep a lot of the time but when they're awake they're demanding of your attention, especially if there's only one and you've got no cage to keep it contained.

I picked one of the hobs, not the biggest, but one I'd worked with enough to have a sense of his habits and temperament.

"Mind you, don't give it a name," Banta said. "That will only confuse you. It's a tool, like a barrow or a spade."

Banta had told me early on that when he started working with ferrets he'd named them and that made it harder when they died. A working ferret has a short life — rats will fight if they're cornered and wounds fester. Sometimes ferrets just sicken for no apparent reason; but refusing to name his ferrets was just what Banta told himself. After I was with him a few months I realized that he'd named them all without realizing it — the different sounds he made when he handled them were their names. We all create fictions about ourselves.

I acquired a horse from a stable outside the city walls. In one of those stableman jokes that you don't appreciate until you're too far from the stable to do anything about it, the horse was called *Steðefæst*. The ostler was on Brorda's payroll and supplied them for hire to the general public and for free to Brorda's operatives, so we often got his dregs.

Banta said goodbye to his ferret and waived me off with a dismissive grunt. At his most personable, Banta was a misanthropic turd. I think he would have preferred it if I'd come to him unnamed as well.

Steðefæst began to show his true colors in the middle of the morning, when he shied unaccountably as we trotted along an empty road. I almost lost my seat, and it took me a minute of struggle to regain control. The horse stood quietly for a while, offering no more indications that he had a concern in the world, and then we continued at the same pace as before, but I was much more tense and wary. I intended to make the ride in easy stages, but it started raining hard the second morning, just after I'd crossed the Tamesis into the country of the East Saxons, and toward the end of a wet and unpleasant day in the saddle I came on a priory at Wokenduna, a satellite dependency of Súþminster, built on land bequeathed by some rich woman contemplating her eventual death and trying to hedge her spiritual bet.

These little foundations are everywhere, sometimes with only two or three monks or nuns, sometimes with more, and you never know when you're going to turn a corner in the road and stumble over a small, dry-masonry oratory, or a hardscrabble religious settlement.

At first the monks weren't overly welcoming, viewing me as just another transient mouth to feed. Their endowment was an odd one, stipulating the production of twenty wheels of cheese *per annum*, and they had a herd of thirty cows and twice as many goats, so they could sustain themselves as cheese makers. Their dairy barn was bigger and better appointed than their chapel and the buildings they lived in, and I traded a couple of hours of ratting for supper and a night's sleep. I set out the nets and released the ferret into the foundations of the barn, and we killed eighteen rats; after that I was as welcome as a royal land grant and the remission of the three duties. The ferret and I had a warm bed by the fire and a hot meal, and we enjoyed our evening of ratting celebrity and ate as much good cheese as we wanted.

The ferret didn't care for it much, so I ate his share.

The ferret was inquisitive, as they all are, and bored, as a lone ferret without the playful diversions of ferret society can easily become, so he explored every crevice in the abbey hall and killed a few mice for sport, further delighting the monk who looked after the cheese stores. The priory was too small to have their division of labor elevated by grand sounding titles. Everyone pitched in to do the work and everyone prayed together, ate together, and slept together, and I couldn't help thinking that it was closer to what Benedict had in mind when he wrote his Rule than the goings on at the lavish houses that Wilfrið had founded everywhere he went, mostly so he could live in the princely style he believed he deserved.

Before I left early the next morning I turned the ferret loose in the dairy foundations one more time, which resulted in another dozen dead rats and a dairy master so grateful that he insisted I accept a wheel of fresh cheese that was almost big enough to mount on the axel of a small cart.

"We don't make that hard cheese that crumbles when you look at it, or that soft cheese that runs like an open sore; we make a nice firm cheese that feels like a young woman's ass." The monastic cheese maker still drew on his secular beginnings for product descriptions, his eyes closed as if he were describing an image floating behind the lids, and I wondered whether he was seeing a wheel of cheese or a naked ass. Whatever image he was reviewing in his mind's eye, the distinction seemed to occupy a warm spot in his heart, and the cheese was good, so I thanked him and rode away. It would make a good contribution to the menu at the wedding feast, and he had plenty to spare — *Þrimilce-mōnaþ* was just past, the month of milking your cows three times a day, the busiest time of their year, and there was hardly room in his cellar for all the cheese wheels.

After my stop at Wokenduna, I pressed hard to make up the time, so there was no more ferreting. I began to discover a pattern to *Steðefæst's* apparently random attempts to unseat me: the horse didn't like running water. But another layer in the onion of its perversity was that not all running water provoked it. There are half a dozen big rivers between Cantwarabyrig and Elmet — the Medway, the Themes, the Great Ouse, the Nene, the Witham, the Trent — but it wasn't the big waters that panicked the horse, it was the small brooks, pools, streams, and puddles, and it wasn't all of them. So, because there was a lot of running water on the trip (the most direct route was through the western fens) I was tense most of the time. That *Steðefæst* only managed to throw me three times and that I didn't break any bones was what a gullible believer would think miraculous.

Loneliness is an awful thing, and I was glad my brother Mæl had found someone to share his life with. He was getting older, and we all hoped that marriage would have a settling effect on him, tempering his attitude and just making him easier to live with in general because, goddamn, he could be a struggle to get along with. Love is sometimes the transformative event that accomplishes a man's metamorphosis. Sometimes not. It had been for me, and in my brother's case, as in mine, the woman he'd chosen had chosen him first, so I took that as a hopeful sign. Among other things, Mæl's name can mean "measure," like an ingredient in a recipe, and it's a family joke that a little bit of Mæl goes a long way.

My family had been trying to fix a date for the wedding since I'd left Elmet a year ago. Initially, both families had resisted the match on grounds of temperament — the problem being that Mæl and Æthelwaru had very similar temperaments, and both kindreds worried that one of them would kill the other, creating a shitestorm of legal and extra-legal reprisals that would rapidly degenerate into a blood feud and sow generations of lethal discord.

Last spring, when I was in Eoforwic after Oswith died, the patriarch of a kingworthy Northumbrian kindred took it into his head that I'd murdered his son. My friends and I had been running a dice game patronized by young *gesith-men — geoguth* idiots who needed someone to wipe their chins for them — and the boy had won big and turned up dead the next morning, so of course they assumed we'd killed him because he won our coin. In fact, most of the coin he won had belonged to his mates, and my best guess was that his own brother had killed him for the same fratricidal motive that's prompted brothers to kill one another since Genesis 4:8, but the Northumbrians (being Northumbrians) wanted a spectacular demonstration of Northumbrian justice, so they picked me and my friends to punish because we were convenient foreigners without oath helpers, who were inhabiting the shadows on the edge of the Law.

Even though the Northumbrian *witangemót* cleared me in the end when I delivered up the real killers (a narrow squeak that was), the dead boy's father refused to accept that I was innocent because he couldn't bring himself to admit that his living son had murdered his dead son. After I left Eoforwic, he sent a dozen killing *thegns* south to get me, and, in an ill advised visit to my *tún*, they'd surprised Mæl and Æthelwaru in a postcoital lull at the tail end of a long afternoon spent focking like Gaulish bunnies. My children were cleaning out the buildings that had been closed when I left for my extended drinking binge in Northumbria after their mother's death, and Mæl was supposed to be watching them. I wasn't at home; I was returning from what I'd thought was my last *gemót* as Sentwine's assistant.

The killing *thegns* underestimated Mæl, assuming that a bruised, tired-looking man with a limp was a soft target. They were all mounted and Mæl was slumped in a doorway, so maybe he looked smaller than he is. They discovered their mistake when they attacked. Even wounded and in a dreamy, post-coital droop, Mæl was a match for any twelve Northumbrians — and then Æthelwaru had appeared, naked, screaming, and swinging an axe. What a chilling sight *that* must have been. Two of the killing *thegns* survived their miscalculation, but one of them grabbed up my son, Young Torhtmund, on his way out, so we had to follow them into Northumbria to get him back.

Æthelwaru had refused to part from Mæl on the grounds that he needed her help because of his depleted condition, and she went with us. She distinguished herself in the bloodbath that followed, and personally recovered my son. After that, my kindred dropped their objections to the marriage. Not her kindred, though; when they learned she'd gone to Northumbria they used it as a pretense to harden their hearts further. Her father accused us of recklessly putting her in danger, even though coming along had been her idea — it certainly wasn't ours.

Her father knew her better than we did, and his resistance to the match was puzzling. I'd seen her at home, and I knew what a formidable disciplinary nightmare she was. I'd have thought he'd be happy to marry her off. But I suppose it came down to the simple fact that a married woman is still the legal responsibility of her kindred; if she lost her temper and filleted Mæl in a fit of rage it would be up to them to compose the killing. Their reluctance might even be viewed as a deep respect for her skills and close combat technique. Having seen the results of her fighting prowess on my *tún* and witnessed her in action in Northumbria, I understood completely.

Whatever the real reason, her kindred adamantly refused to permit the marriage for so long that I was beginning to think it would never happen unless Mæl took her by force, and then they suddenly relented and permitted the *hand-fæstung*. No one seemed to know the reason; it was yet another mystery among all the other mysteries that enveloped my brother's love life.

Even after the *hand-fæstung* her father haggled obstinately over the bride price — the monetary compensation to the kindred for the lost productivity of his daughter — and he insisted on a ridiculous amount. Once, handfasting was both a declaration of intent and an act of binding together, but as the influence of the Church grew the importance of the religious ceremony increased, as did the fees and payments that came to the Church in connection with the formal observance of the sacrament, the declaration of handfast had become preliminary to the marriage, and the marriage ceremony itself couldn't take place until the bride price was established.

Hard-nosed bargaining followed; offers and counter-offers were exchanged like volleys of arrows in a battle that lasted through the autumn and past Christmas into the New Year. When two kindreds want a marriage, the time between hand-fasting and wedding is as short as possible, but Æthelwaru's kindred most demonstrably did not want the marriage. I followed the negotiations at a distance through my correspondence with Creda, the advocate to the Elmetsætan *witan* and my first teacher of Law.

Creda handled the marriage settlement as a favor to me. It was an acknowledgement of my sacrifice in the service of continued Elmetsætan autonomy. I don't know how many versions of the marriage contract he drafted before both families agreed on the wording and the content, but the tone of Creda's letters took on a more frustrated edge throughout the prolonged negotiations. Finally he succeeded in brokering the deal, and the bans were posted on the door of the Minster church in Loidis. Thanks to our rambling tour of the *Andrade Weald*, by the time I read Creda's letter in Cantwarabyrig I had only two weeks to make the trip home. And now, as I sat on *Steðefæst*, waiting for a final, unprovoked convulsion and looking at old Torhtmund's *tún* across ploughed furlongs and meadows and the enclosed home field from the high ground that overlooked the hidage, I'd finally arrived.

The Dog Man

The Dog Man sat on a barrel surrounded by his flea-ridden pack and watched the newly-arrived guests attempt to pitch their tents, remembering exactly why he preferred the company of dogs to humans. In the last five minutes alone the thud of mallets on tent pegs had three times been interrupted by screams and curses as men, made inattentive by drink, had hammered their own hands. Guests who were already in place were greeting new arrivals with horns of mead and cups of beer. It would be another loud night and difficult to get to sleep.

He reached down and patted the head of the closest dog, which was scratching its ear with a hind leg. The dog made a sound in its throat and thumped its tail twice on the ground. Then the Dog Man saw a single horseman ride down the slope into the home field from the south west. He didn't recognize the horse, and at that distance the man was just a man in the saddle of the walking horse. Behind the Dog Man there was a loud shout as someone tripped over a guy rope and fell on his face. The rope thrummed like a harp string as the man got to his knees and took stock of his injuries, although he seemed more concerned that he'd spilled whatever he'd been drinking. He retrieved the cup from where it had rolled, and then he got slowly to his feet.

"Christ," the Dog Man said to his dogs. The dogs knew what he meant.

The rider was now off the slope of the hill and crossing the home field, but some of the tents pitched obscured the Dog Man's view. He got off the barrel and the dogs stood up expectantly. There was something familiar about the rider, but before the Dog Man could place him, one of the wedding guests walked up and all tail wagging stopped.

"Firewood," the man said.

"What about it?" the Dog Man asked.

"Is there any?"

"There is if you brought it with you." The Dog Man wasn't a *tún-geréfa*, and he saw no reason why it was the responsibility of Torhtmund's people to provide the basics of life for these freeloaders. The wedding was still a week away.

The man seemed to think that the Dog Man was being rude, and he stepped forward to make some sharp remark, but nine dogs closed around him in a low hum of warning growls. They were all waiting for some indication from the Dog Man that they should just take this inebriated shite weasel down in his tracks and savage him until he apologized for the sorry state of his life. The Dog Man considered giving them the nod, but thought the better of it and whistled them off. The man lost interest in firewood and wandered away.

Hring

The wedding was almost a week away and yet the enclosed area of Old Torhtmund's tún and, as well as the meadow outside the gate, were already dotted with clusters of tents and canopies like mushrooms in a pasture. The temporary pavilion that would house the wedding feast was under construction in the center of the home field; posts were sunk into the earth and beams and trusses were being set into place.

I recognized the familiar outlines of the structure taking shape. All of Old Torhtmund's children had their wedding feasts in a huge rectangular pavilion in the home field. Its length could be extended or reduced to suit the number of guests. When it was finished it have three stone hearths distributed along the center axis, flanked by guest tables, so the celebration would have sufficient light and heat to last through the night. The pavilion would have a thatched roof and a board floor and no walls. Generally, a wedding feast would be held in the house or hall of the household hosting the ceremony, but the size of this gathering would burst Old Torhtmund's hall at the seams.

An acre of the home field was fenced off and a small herd of horses milled in the enclosure. Waggons and carts were lined up against the home field wall. The home field boar had been driven into a stone enclosure to keep it safely out of the way, and the guests tossed their garbage and food scraps into the temporary sty. Cooking fires exhaled columns of smoke into the evening air and there was already a festival feeling about the encampment. I nudged *Steðefæst* into motion and rode down the slope.

When I passed through the gate ten minutes later, it was clear to me that Mæl's wedding, despite the reluctance of the bride's kindred, was going to rival one of the old pagan fire festivals in size. The early arrivals had festooned the trees inside the *tún* wall with streamers and hung lanterns with shaved horn panels from limbs. I reckoned there would be jugglers and harpists and singers and a universally jubilant mood. There were already at least fifty scattered tents and no one paid any attention to me as I dismounted at the barn and unsaddled my horse. Like the rest of the amenities inside the walls of the *tún*, the stable was reserved for Old Torhtmund's use, and there were a couple of empty stalls. I set the saddle on an empty limb of the saddle tree and hung the padding over the top board of the stall to dry. I put a little grain and some fresh grass in the feed trough before I started grooming the horse.

I ached every time I moved, stiff from the accumulated tension of anticipating a sudden convulsion from *Steðefæst* that only seemed to come if I relaxed my vigilance. It had been a long ride, but it was good to finish it with the repetitive activity of brushing down a tired horse, combing out its mane, and picking the dirt out of its hooves because it gave me time to prepare myself to see my family again.

When I was finished grooming and feeding the horse, I put the bag that contained the sleeping ferret over my shoulder and walked to the hall. I hadn't gone twenty paces before a voice called out: "Saint Peter's bleeding piles I thought that looked like you. I'm glad you're here. This wedding's been a nightmare from start to finish."

I stopped in my tracks and turned around as six or eight tail-wagging dogs boiled around my legs and the Dog Man walked up, shaking his head in disbelief.

The Dog Man didn't seem to have changed since I'd seen him last except he was due for his seasonal haircut. The dogs began to show interest in the smell of ferret clinging to the bag over my shoulder, but they must have put it down to another of my eccentricities because they shifted their attention to me and began to smell the backs of my knees and my feet and my crotch and my fists and my ass as they added me to the catalogue of things they weren't supposed to attack, at least for the time being, then they dropped into the dirt and waited to see what their master wanted to do next.

The Dog Man embraced me, and I reckoned it would take a day or so in the open air to get rid of the transferred dog hair and the smell of damp mutt. One of the dogs took a long deep sniff of the contents of the sack and looked at the Dog Man and said, "Woof?"

"What's in the bag?" the Dog Man asked.

"A ferret."

"Dead?"

"Of course not dead. Why would I have a dead ferret in a bag?"

"You'd have a good reason," he shrugged. "Ferret's a good animal for you," he said. "Noses into tight spaces and dark holes and flushes out rats. What are you doing with a ferret?"

"I've spent the last year learning to work ferrets."

"Something useful at last," he laughed. "How long are you staying?"

"A couple of weeks."

The Dog Man nodded and spat as a small crowd of wedding guests jostled us when they walked unsteadily by, talking loudly and pulling at jugs of beer or cider or mead — some liquid that made them lightheaded and soft-kneed and heedless of courtesy.

"They've been showing up every couple of

hours since yesterday morning," the Dog Man said. "Can't get naught done. And they all want free advice about their dogs, like there's some secret to a well-trained dog beside hard work, the lazy shites."

"Where's the family?"

"Torhtmund and Flæd are in the hall. Your brothers and sisters are all keeping clear until the wedding."

If I wanted to see my brothers and sisters before the wedding, I'd have to go to them because I knew them well enough to know that they'd avoid the increasingly-chaotic festivity on Old Torhtmund's *tún*. It looked like the entire population of the hundred would be celebrating my brother's marriage.

"It's going to be a feast as hasn't been seen in the hundred for a long time," the Dog Man continued, as if he were reading my mind. "Torhtmund's been laying in beer and mead for two months."

"I expect there won't be a drop left," I said. "I better get to the hall before it's all gone."

The Dog Man rallied his mutts with a sharp whistle and set off wherever he'd been heading when he saw me.

Sprot

S **prot walked by** the place in the shambles where the killing *thegn* had tried to gut him two years before and looked down at the pavement where he'd left the eviscerated bastard bleeding out. Sprot always thought about the dead killing *thegn* when he passed the spot between two butcher stalls, one specializing in mutton, the other in pork. The pavement was mottled with a brown bloodstain—unremarkable in the shambles, one fading bloodstain among many, but a significant bloodstain for Sprot because he knew that except for luck it could have been his.

The killing *thegn* had been waiting to ambush him, pretending to browse the hanging quarters of mutton, but Sprot had chanced to notice him watching and then saw him look away as Sprot met his eye, his face half hidden by a hanging side of pork in the neighboring stall, then Sprot saw the killing *thegn*'s hand move to his knife, and in that moment when he was obscured by the side of pork Sprot, lunged forward, shouldering it into the killing *thegn* and knocking him backward into the counter of the stall.

The struggle had been brief and bloody and ended four seconds later with the killing *thegn* on his back and his ropy, blue-hued guts oozing out of a deep belly slash and over his thighs onto the pavement, the stench of bile and hemorrhaged blood and partially-digested food drifting up from the perforations and rents left by Sprot's deft blade work. Sprot knelt on his arm and removed the killing *thegn's* knife from his fingers. He could see in the man's eyes that he knew he was dying.

"Who are you?" Sprot asked.

The killing *thegn* grimaced as Sprot shifted his weight, but he said nothing. Sprot reached down and held up a steaming handful of the man's bleeding intestines for him to see.

"If you want me to send for a priest," Sprot said. "Tell me who you are."

"Osbald sent me," he said.

Sprot looked around at the gathered faces, always quick to assemble and curious to see a man die. "Send for a priest and the gate *geréfas*," he said.

Sprot always relived that killing when he walked past the spot because he always thought: *what if I'd been looking somewhere else? What if I hadn't noticed him watching me?*

Then he was past the butchers' stalls and nodding to acknowledge some men who'd recognized him and called out a greeting; Sprot had become a celebrity in the shambles because of that killing.

The Frisian had sent word he wanted to see Sprot.

Sprot had a confusing history with this particular Frisian, called Rud. When he'd first come to Sprot's attention it had been because of a murder, and Sprot had organized and led the squad that tried to arrest him and his brother, Radbod, and their friend from Elmet, a man called Hring, in a barn where he'd been sleeping off the previous night's revels. Sprot's immediate superior, sensing an opportunity for advancement, had taken command at the last minute and bungled the apprehension. In the confusion, Sprot had found himself chasing Hring through the shambles, up the hill, through the gate, and then to the *frith* seat in the minster cathedral.

That had been at the beginning of Lent a year before the one just passed. Since then, Sprot had been in disgrace with his superiors, then out of disgrace, then a lesser hero among his fellow *geréfas*, then sent south with a warning and Hring's *wergeld*, then set upon and beaten by Hring's brothers, then feted like an honored guest in Hring's father's *tún*, then involved in the rescue of a former Mercian queen-become-abbess in Elmet, then a blood rider in a raid on a *tún* west of Catræth, and finally promoted to his former superior's position. And most of that had been in the company of the Frisian Rud and his brother Rad-bod and Hring; men he would have been only too happy to hang when he'd first met them.

Sprot had never been particularly philosophical, but he sensed that some greater force he didn't understand had noticed him and decided to turn his life into a series of bewildering japes for its own amusement.

Sprot crossed the bridge that spanned the Foss and angled into the trading *wic*, where men were speaking Frisian, several Frankish dialects, Norse, Hebrew, Gaul, and even Walloon—like a living lesson about the Tower of Babble. He turned right, deeper into the *wic*, then left, and then he saw the warehouse that belonged to Rud's father, Gisl.

Radbod was working in the small area in the front. "Sprot," he called out. "How have you been?"

"Well enough," the *geréfa* answered, glancing through the open door of the warehouse. "Your brother sent word that he wanted to talk to me."

"Have you heard from Hring?"

"He was in Wessex last I knew."

"His brother Mæl is getting married in a few weeks."

"I've had word. We're invited to the wedding."

"That's what we wanted to see you about. We're taking a couple of waggons, and we can add another if you want to travel with us."

"Somerild's insisting on going," Sprot said. "And a waggon would let us take the children in better comfort. Thanks."

"It's settled then," Radbod smiled.

Of the two brothers, Radbod was the one that people warmed to. A naturally personable man, able to deal with anyone, he was the one who did business with the customers at the warehouse. Rud was less voluble and more volatile. In charge of cataloguing and maintaining the inventory, he occupied himself with bills of lading and tracking the inventory on hand.

"Is Rud here?"

"He's arranging a wedding present for Hring's brother."

"What is it?"

"Something that came to our father from a colleague of his in Quentovic. He thought we might be able to sell it to the king, but when Rud saw it, he decided nothing else would do for Mæl's wedding gift."

Mæl and his woman had been on the raid to Catræth last year, together with the Frisian brothers, Hring's nephew Ordgar, and the entire complement of *geréfas* from the advocate's *hird* that Hring had been a part of in Elmet. Even the chaplain had come. It wasn't a ride that Sprot was likely to forget, and everyone who had been there was connected in a way that only men who had spilled blood together could be.

"Is it a secret?"

"Just a surprise. I'll show you." Radbod started into the warehouse and Sprot followed him.

Dring

There were smaller pavilions and canopies scattered through the trees, roped to trunks and branches and supported by poles and guy lines, and the *folc* were eating and drinking in the shade. I'd been to *witangemóts* that had less infrastructure and organization.

There were scatters of laughter and a few people recognized me under my beard and I acknowledged them with a smile and a wave, but I wanted a bath and a change of clothes and a good night's sleep, not the society of freeloading drunks arguing raucously about the location of something that seemed vital at the moment but that they'd soon forget about.

At the head of a small reception line inside the house, Old Torhtmund was accepting the good wishes of his arriving guests and Flæd was dipping them a starter cup of mead. I was going to take my place at the end of the line and surprise them, but they saw me as I came through the door and broke the protocol of wedding hospitality by abandoning the reception line to greet me. There was plenty of time for them to make small talk with wedding guests; we hadn't seen each other in a year.

I'd been writing to them in care of Creda, and he occasionally mentioned that he'd passed a letter along, but since neither of them was literate, I'd had no replies. Except for their trip to Northumbria to give me to the church twenty-one winters ago, neither of them had ever left Elmet, so my letters must have seemed like coded reports arriving erratically from the edge of the known world. My father nearly crushed me with his embrace; my mother's was less overwhelming but no less fierce.

"We've missed you," Old Torhtmund said.

"I've missed you. Are the preparations complete?"

"Nearly."

"How many guests are coming?"

"Everyone Mæl's ever insulted," my mother laughed.

"Everyone he's ever met, then. Do you think there's room enough? You've only got twenty-five hides, and some of them are under the plough."

"It could be tight," my father admitted.

"We're giving them the first drink," Flæd said looking back to the small group of men and women that they'd abandoned when they saw me. "After that, they have to shift for themselves."

"Where are the children?"

"On your *tún*," Old Torhtmund said.

"Sentwine found a *geréfa* to run the hidage, and Eadgiþ's back from the convent. She's taking care of them."

That was a surprise. Eadgiþ was my youngest sister, and she'd gone to a convent when she was fifteen, despite my considered advice. She'd been disappointed in love and thought that the answer to her unhappiness lay in a nun's life. There was nothing anyone could do about it, she was of an age to make up her own mind, and so Old Torhtmund had donated half a hide as a profession gift and taken her and a symbolic sod to the abbey of St. Mildgyth, a small foundation that was happy enough to accept even the sister of a well-known apostate in exchange for 70 timbered acres.

"They gave her leave to attend the wedding?"

"Much the same kind of leave they gave you."

Since my leave of absence had been the un-sought, permanent kind, it seemed that none of Old Torhtmund's children were destined for the religious life. Whatever had happened, I'm sure that her return hadn't been easy, although I'd already put Old Torhtmund through the inconvenient turmoil of reintegrating someone who'd left the Church back into the kindred, so he had the experience.

When I'd come back from Eoforwic, Eadgiþ had been alive eight winters, the same age I'd been when I was given to the minster. She'd be nineteen winters now, and living on her own on my *tún* — a literate, disgruntled professional virgin watching over my children. What could go wrong with that?

Ordgar

I **stood up from the milking stool** and lifted the
bucket to the table outside the stall. Then I un-
tied the white cow and turned her into the
small fenced enclosure next to the barn. There
were two white cows on the *tún*; the others in the
small herd were still in the west pasture. The stall
needed mucking, but that wasn't my problem. I
was willing to milk a cow, but my father bred and
trained oxen, so there was mucking enough waiting for me at home. I was taking my turn at
Hring's *tún* to help Eadgiþ with the children. All
the older cousins took their turn on Hring's *tún*
while he was gone in the south, and none of us resented the extra work.

Last year, Hring had taken me on what turned
out to be his last *gemót* in the south of Elmet, and
what had started out to be a boring trip had
turned into something that I'd never be able to
forget even if I wanted to, and right after that, I

went with him into Northumbria to get my young cousin Torhtmund back. I still dream about what happened in Northumbria sometimes, but I never talk about it. What is there to say? Who would understand that wasn't there?

In some ways I was closer to Hring's children than to my own brothers and sisters; I'd spilled blood for them twice before I was old enough to get my iron.

Even though Eadgiþ was my mother's sister, she was only three years older than me, and we'd been children together. She was six months back from a convent and living on Hring's *tún* and minding his children while she collected herself. I'd been sorry when she'd gone into the convent and happy to see her again when she came back.

I picked up the milk bucket and left the barn.

The *tún* was quiet as evening came on and the two families of *ceorls*, a shepherd and a plough-man, their work finished for the day, prepared their evening meals. It was quiet in that end-of-the-day way things get quiet when all the work's done, the tired kind of quiet. Cooking smoke that smelled of oak and burnt gravy and underdone meat hung among the trees. The sheep bleated in the fold and one of the dogs barked.

I glanced over the wall and saw a man walking alone across the home field toward the *tún*. I stopped and watched him come, setting the bucket on the ground and walking closer to the gate for a better look in the gathering dusk. Strangers coming to a *tún* just before nightfall make me nervous. We'd come to that *tún* in Northumbria just about this time of day. I thought about going to get my bow, but he'd be at the gate before I could get back with an arrow on the bowstring. I gripped the handle of my *seax*. The wall of the *tún* was only chest high, so I had an unobstructed view as he got closer. He was wearing a dark cloak and carrying a bag over his shoulder. He was bearded and his hood was up. Although there was something familiar about him, I couldn't place him until he was closer, when he pushed his hood back and brushed the shaggy hair out of his eyes in a familiar gesture that I recognized.

I waited by the gate, and when Hring was still a couple of rods away I lifted the bar and pushed it open, stepping out into the field.

"Ordgar," Hring said as we embraced.

We held onto each other for a long moment, not saying anything, not having to. It felt good seeing him again. It was more than the usual strong bond between someone and his mother's brother. My mother had a lot of brothers, and I saw them frequently, but we'd never been through what Hring and I had been through together.

"You look well. Are you just getting back?"

"I stopped at Old Torhtmund's, first" he said. "How are the children?"

"Come and see." I motioned him through the open gate.

"What are you doing here?"

"I come by every couple of days to see if Eadgiþ needs help." I picked up the milk bucket.

"How is Eadgiþ?"

"Glad to be out of the convent."

Hring opened the door and walked into the long house. The roof thatch held the heat from the fire, and it was warm and a little smoky inside and the smell the evening meal, simmering in the pot that hung from the rafter over the hearth, made me realize that I was hungry. The table was haphazardly set in half a dozen places, the usual clutter when Hring's youngest daughter Osgiva helped. Empty bowls waited for whatever was simmering in the pot and two loaves of bread on a plate and a pot of butter and a pot of honey were waiting on the table beside the salt cellar.

"Look who I found at the gate," I said.

There was a moment's hesitation as Hring and his children took a breath; I reckoned they were using that moment of recognition to get used to the difference between their memories of each other and how they looked now — Hring a winter older, bearded and hardened from tramping through the south and sleeping rough and ready under hedges; my cousins a winter older, bigger, faces suddenly different and yet the same in their father's eyes, sleeping warm and safe and tucked up in their own beds.

The children hesitated, maybe because it took them a second to recognize their father under his beard. He must have seemed even more a stranger to them. He carried himself like a man who walked more than he rode, and who worked with his hands and not his head. They sensed the difference in him, and they were struggling to understand what it was. Hring took off the leather bag and hung it on a hook on one of the posts that supported the rafters.

There was a strange awkwardness to his homecoming. After what had happened in Northumbria, I didn't doubt his love for his children, but none of them had seen the proof of it. They only remembered that he'd left them when their mother died and stayed away for nearly a year. They remembered that he'd come back with promises never to leave again, and then broken those promises and gone south for another year. Two years is a long time when you're small, and they were too small to understand why either of those leavings had happened, but they were big enough to suffer because of them, and to be wary of the returns.

I set the bucket of milk on the table and looked at Eadgiþ, who was standing back in the twisting red firelight by the end of the hearth. She hadn't seen her brother since she left for the convent, but she kept silent as Hring knelt down and his children slowly came to him. He opened his arms to embrace them all together and they accepted the embrace with a sad reluctance. Sometimes they asked me about him, if I knew where he was and when he might be coming back, and I told them what we all told them, that he'd gone away to serve Elmet and the kindred, and so they would be safe, but I knew they didn't understand it. I'm not sure that Hring understood it.

"You've gotten older," he said. "That's what happens when I'm not around to watch you."

His voice was thick, but he didn't seem aware of it.

"We'd get older even if you were here," Young Torhtmund said.

"True, but it would be harder to notice." Hring sat back on his heels and looked at his children. "You're all bigger."

He looked at them for a long moment. "I missed you all so much."

The children didn't seem to know what to say to that.

"Hello Hring." Eadgiþ said when the pause had gotten uncomfortably long. "Have I gotten older too?"

Hring looked up at his sister standing shadowy by the hearth.

I sat down on the bench. In the last year I'd become more of an observer. Last summer at St. Werburga in the Weald I found out that you can learn more when you keep your mouth shut and your eyes open. That was when I met the *geréfas* that Hring had worked with on the *gemót* circuit. And the Cantwara girl, Uda.

Hring stood up to greet his sister. At that angle I could see the firelight reflect for a brief instant on his wet cheeks above his beard.

"You're looking well," he said. "The avowed life not agreeable after all?"

"The prioress was a stupid bitch," Eadgiþ said. "She was going to put me in an anchorite's cell because I questioned her judgment."

"Not *you*, surely."

They held one another for a long moment, and it seemed to me that the fierceness of that wordless holding was their way of saying what they couldn't say out loud.

"Oh, no, there was plenty questionable about her judgment," Eadgiþ said when they broke the embrace. "I was just the only one with iron enough to ask the questions."

"I seem to remember something about a vow of obedience," he said.

"I was obedient for the first couple of winters," she said. "Prayed and fasted and mortified the flesh, gave up eating meat and pretended to like turnip gruel. I even learned to read and write. But the prioress had no idea how to run a milking shed let alone a convent. She pissed away the purse and ran the convent toward a cliff. Wouldn't take advice from anyone."

"Meaning you?"

"Meaning anyone."

"Wasn't she elected to the position?"

"Not by me." Eadgiþ uncovered the cider barrel and dipped a cup. "*Wassail*, brother," she said as she approached, offering him the drink. "Welcome home."

"Good apple harvest?" Hring asked, accepting the cup.

"Better than the year before," I said as Hring took his first sip. "We've a good few barrels of scrumpy laid by."

I knew that the cider was good — tart and strong and barrel-hardened — two-cup cider that would leave your head swimming if you drank it too fast.

The children had taken themselves a little apart while Hring and Eadgiþ talked. Mæthild, the oldest, had her arm around her little sister Osgiva. Young Torhtmund and his little brother Gulhere were sitting on the hearth with their backs to the fire. They were all watching their father and their aunt, and I wondered if they weren't curious about how they should be feeling about his return and looking to Eadgiþ for direction.

The bag that Hring had hung on the post began to squirm. There was something in it that was alive and wanted out, and then a small masked face pushed out from under the unsecured flap and a ferret shook its head and sneezed. Gulhere saw it immediately and went over and stood underneath it, and he and the ferret looked at each other curiously.

Hring went over and opened the flap and reached out a ferret. He took out a long leather lead and snapped it to the leather harness around the animal's front legs and set it on the ground, tying the end to the post. The ferret sneezed again and shook its head in a rapid blur as the children crowded around, but Hring warned them back.

"He's got sharp teeth and he isn't slow to use them," he said.

"Is he for us?" Osgiva asked.

"What's his name?" Mæthild wanted to know.

"No, he helps me catch rats, and he doesn't have a name. He's just ferret. After we eat I'll turn him loose in here, and we'll see if he can't get a mouse or two."

"Are you home for good?" Mæthild asked her father in a voice that was smaller than her usual voice, as if she didn't want the question answered.

I could see that the children didn't know what to feel. I knew they wanted their father, despite everything that had happened between them, but I reckon they were afraid to hear him say he was staying because they were afraid it wasn't true, no matter what the answer was.

"Only for a while. I have to go back after Mæl's wedding," he told her.

When Oswith died, Hring left his children with his mother and father and spent the autumn and winter after Oswith's death drinking and gambling in Eoforwic, where he'd gone to school, except this time he studied dice and drunkenness instead of God and Latin. Mæl said that Oswith's death had hit him so hard that it knocked clear out of his old life.

Some in the kindred, Derehild's side, had revived all that shite about his being expelled from the minster in the first place. I thought that going off to drink and forget made sense when Oswith died. My mother, Enflæda, was close to Hring and Oswith, and growing up I'd spent almost as much time on their *tún* as my own. My mother had been so gob-smacked by Oswith's death that she stopped working around the *tún* for nearly three months — the house had gone to shite while she just walked alone in the wintry fields crying. It had been frightening.

After what had happened last summer, I thought I understood loss a little better and Hring a little more, and then the Mercians said they wanted Hring to work for them and there was nothing for it. Instead of getting back his life with his children Hring had to go south.

Since then I'd become a kind of big brother to my cousins, especially the boys, Torhtmund and Gulhere, who I taught to shoot a bow. They were easy with me, not guarded about the confused way they felt about Hring. They loved him and they hated him, too. I thought it was good sign that they felt his absence at all. Hring had promised he'd never leave again, but the Mercians made a liar out of him on that score. They didn't care a bishop's fart what promises he'd made to his children or what it meant to break them.

Hring knelt down so he was at their eye level.

"I'd stay forever if it was down to me," he said. "I'd never leave again. But I told you that before and then the Mercians made me go south."

"We talked about this," Eadgiþ took the empty cup from Hring.

"Can I go with you when you leave?" Torhtmund asked. I was surprised, and I could see that Hring was surprised, too. Torhtmund was an eager boy, and it wouldn't be out of place for a ratcatcher to have a boy his age along. I wondered if Hring would consider it.

"I depend on you to look after you brother and sisters," Hring told him. "By the time they're old enough to do without you, I'll be done with this job and back home and neither of us will have to leave the hundred ever again."

"I want to leave the hundred," Torhtmund said. "You left. Eadgiþ left. Ordgar left. Why can't I?"

"You can do what you want when you're of age," Hring said.

"I want to come too," Gulhere said.

"You think you're old enough to come?"

"I *am* four winters old," he said.

Hring took a deep breath and refused to smile.

"You're both getting pretty big," Hring admitted. "But the law says you're not men until you get your iron when you're fifteen, and you can't be *sundornotu-geréfas* until you're of age. There's nothing I can do about it. How would it look for an advocate to break the law?"

"You're not an advocate anymore," Young Torhtmund said.

I don't know if Young Torhtmund had wanted to be cruel when he said that, but I saw Hring blink, and then he said, "I'm bound by law the same as everyone."

"Food's ready," Eadgiþ said, removing the pot from the hook and carrying it to the table. "Mæthild, get another bowl for Hring. And you two—come eat before you start packing."

We all sat down at the table and Eadgiþ ladled out the meal while the children asked questions about where Hring had been and what he'd seen and done.

"Mostly we just go from place to place and kill rats," he said.

"What kind of places?"

"Monasteries and *feorm* barns and granaries and mills," he said.

"Don't they have ratcatchers in Mercia?"

"That's not all we do," he said. "When we're in the scriptoriums we look at what they're working on, charters and wills and things like that. Sometimes we copy them, if the Mercians want us to."

"It sounds like fun," Gulhere said.

"It never felt like fun," Hring told him.

"What would happen if they caught you?" Eadgiþ asked.

"We'd have a time explaining how ratcatchers can read and write."

Hring glossed over that part of it. I reckon if they'd been caught he'd have had his skin peeled off until he told them who he worked for. Then a fast death if he was lucky. "Mostly it was boring work," he continued, "sifting for interesting information in the routine documentation of monotonous lives."

He didn't look like an advocate anymore, but he still talked like that. It was all that education — sometimes you almost needed an interpreter.

When they finished eating, the girls showed Hring their work in progress on the loom: a cloak they were making for Mæl as a wedding gift. I'd been watching the cloak take shape on the loom for weeks, and I'd seen every disagreement the two girls had about thread color, design, and execution. They'd already finished Æthelwaru's cloak, and they got it out of the chest to show Hring. The weaving was tight, but the pattern on the hem was somewhat uneven. They were proud, like you are when you accomplish something over your head. Hring praised it and promised them that Æthelwaru and Mæl would treasure their gifts.

Then Hring played a game of *tafl* with Torhtmund while the girls argued about how best to work in the woad-dyed yarn that defined the bottom of the hem. I'd played lots of *tafl* with Torhtmund, and he was always on the attack. Sure enough, Torhtmund tried to break his king out of the defensive middle of the board for the safety of a corner square without covering his flank. Hring explained where he'd gone wrong as he took his pieces from the board. Torhtmund was a good loser. Then Hring had to duel with Gulhere, who'd been practicing with the wooden sword and shield Hring had given him last summer. Gulhere demonstrated his attack against a spearman while Hring defending himself with a broom handle.

Instead of the reckless attack Torhtmund had tried on the *tafl* board, Gulhere was craftier and tried to get Hring to commit himself with a series of feints that he announced beforehand, so his father could admire how much he'd learned. Hring backed away from him beside the hearth, and then tripped backwards, and Gulhere leapt on him and finished him off.

I helped Eadgiþ clean up while Hring's children welcomed him home.

"It's a surprise he's back," Eadgiþ said.

"Mother said he'd come for the wedding if he could." I put the wooden plates in the cupboard. "How long has it been since you've seen him?"

"Four winters. He's changed. He's harder around the eyes."

"That's just since last summer."

Eadgiþ watched her brother play with Gulhere as she cleared the cooking pot and spoons from the hearth. "What was he like when Oswith died?"

I shrugged. "He left the children with Old Torhtmund and went to Eoforwic. Mother says he came back rich, but the enemies he made are richer."

Eadgiþ knew all about the trouble the previous summer and about Hring having to work for the Mercians. She'd left the convent and come to live on his *tún* with the children only a couple of months after Hring had gone south. She told me she was too old to be comfortable living on old Torhtmund's *tún*.

"What happened in Northumbria?" she asked.

"What does Young Torhtmund say?"

"He only knows what happened to him."

"He's little," I said. "There's still a lot of time for him to forget."

Then Hring brought out the ferret and let him sniff along the foundations to see what was living in the house.

"Ferrets do most of their killing underground or in the hollows of walls and under raised floors," Hring told them. "But in a place like this ferret's more likely to flush a rodent ahead of his sharp teeth, so we have to stand ready with willow switches to swat whatever runs away from him."

That turned it into a game, and the children scattered and came back with switches. Hring set them far enough apart that they wouldn't hit each other, on the first swing at least. Soon the ferret flushed a mouse from under the sleeping platforms, and it ran for cover through falling switches that raised a lot of dust and noise but didn't come close to hitting it.

"Careful you don't hurt the ferret," Hring said,

deflecting a hard swing of the willow with the broom stick. "Watch me."

He took a switch and demonstrated how to do it, missing his first swing at the next mouse but killing it with the second. The children got excited and clamored for another mouse, but Hring put an end to the party for the night. They pleaded for just another mouse each before they had to go to the blankets, but he took their switches and sent them to bed.

Eadgiþ made them say a long litany of bedtime prayers to thank God for their father's safe return home. While they were praying, Hring and I went outside to walk the wall and verify that the gate was locked.

"How's the new *tún-geréfa* working out?" Hring asked.

"He's an odd one," I said.

"How so?"

"Likes things a certain way. Makes a fuss if they aren't done exact."

"How's that a bad thing?"

"Eadgiþ would know better than me," I said. He'd find out about the new *geréfa* from her.

Hring was happy to be home, and he strolled slowly as if he were reacquainting himself with the feel of the night.

"Nighttime was always my favorite time to walk around the *tún*," he said. "We used to walk the wall and look out over the still home fields. Sometimes we'd see a deer or a family of wild pigs in the moonlight. Sometimes we'd just watched the stars move across the sky. I used to think about how the same stars have crossed the same sky for thousands of winters and will until the end of time, and how people I've never known and never will know will look at them and think the same thoughts I was thinking."

I knew how he felt. I liked to think about things like that, but I knew better than to talk to anyone about them. If people knew the things I liked to think about they might want to seal me up in a cave. Hring had grown up in the minster in Eoforwic where they spent all their free time talking about stars moving in the sky and how many angels there were in heaven and whether time began with the creation of man, or maybe God Himself was time, and so Time *always* was. One night I'd heard him talking to the priest Jaruman about things like that when I was with the advocate's *hird,* and I'd had bad dreams.

"I used to think God put those thoughts in my head, and I felt the way you feel when you're little and lie in bed before you fall asleep at night trying to comprehend infinity, but then I went to the minster, and after my years at the school in Eoforwic I came to think it was just me noticing celestial mechanics, the way the Greeks had, without any divine inspiration. Now I look at the sky and I just feel alone. Maybe as much because Oswith's underground as because I think the sky's empty of anything but stars."

I didn't know what to say to that, so I didn't say anything. We just stood there looking up at the sky.

"How have the children been?" he asked after a while.

I didn't know what to say to that, either, because I knew he wasn't asking about runny noses and stubbed toes and fevers, but I knew he wanted an answer, so I said, "They don't know what to think of your going away. They want you back, and they don't want you back. They miss you and they don't miss you. Old Torhtmund and Flæd told them you didn't have a choice, and that things would have been bad for everyone if you hadn't gone, so you really went away to keep them safe."

"I don't reckon that makes much difference to them," he said.

We stood there for a long time, looking at the half moon showing through the scattered clouds.

"Soon Mæl and Æthelwaru will look at the sky together," I said. "Last summer I looked at the sky with Uda."

"How have you been keeping? Fancy anyone special?"

"Weddings," I snorted. "They make everyone ask that question."

"Is there an answer?"

"The answer's no," I said.

"The girls must be after you even more than they were last summer."

I wasn't going to answer that one either. I just looked out at the quiet home field and listened to a nightjar trill and whistle in the dark.

"How's working for your father?" he asked after a minute.

"I've only gone on a few trips with him since I got my iron."

"Thought any more about what you prefer?" Hring had been after me to make a future in an advocate's *hird*. I reckon he thought he'd be back when he was finished working for Offa in the south, and he wanted someone to train me up so I could work with him."

"None of the oxen have tried to kill me," I said.

"That's not really an answer."

But it was all the answer he was going to get from me.

Dring

I **was hoping to sleep in**, but when I opened my eyes my children were standing silently beside the bed watching me breathe. It's an unnerving way to wake up, your children looking at you like ravens waiting for you to surrender that last breath so they can get on with dinner. They'd been distant last evening, although they got excited when the ferret was chasing mice, and as soon as I blinked awake they started talking, urging me to get out of bed and eat so we could get started with the ferret again. They had a bundle of switches, fresh cut and stripped of their leaves, all supple as snakes and longer than I am tall. I saw that Young Torhtmund had inscribed some garbled runes into the thick end of a few of them, whether to mark them for his own or imbue them with some supposedly potent anti-rodent magic or just to demonstrate his mastery of the knife I'd given him last year, I'd have to wait for him to reveal.

Gulhere was kitted out with his wooden sword and shield, good defensive thinking in case the rats rose up in a mob against their oppressors and things got ugly. He was small enough that it must seem like a real threat.

Mæthild and Osgiva, who I'd have thought would be more interested in the ferret than killing rats, surprised me by taking up switches (without runes) and positioning themselves on either end of the line, leaving me and their brothers in the middle. I took the hob out of the sack, where he'd been sleeping, and let him sniff around the foundation of the stable. There was a cow and two oxen and three horses in stalls and they produced shite at the usual rate so the manure pile out back was fragrant and as tall as my youngest son, attracting all the verminous attention a manure pile attracts. One of the *ceorls* was mucking the stalls, dumping spadefuls of fresh, warm shite into a barrow while outside another *ceorl* was loading spadefuls of cold, mellowed shite into another barrow to spread around the vegetable garden on the far end of the *tún*. It was like some colloquial poem about the majestic circle of life on the farm — I was a little surprised to discover how much I'd missed it.

The ferret got its bearings and then sniffed along the foundation stones until it found an opening it could get its head into, all a ferret needs by way of an invitation, and then it wriggled out of sight.

"Watch all along the foundation," I said. "Usually I'd have netting over the other holes to catch the rats trying to get away, but I left them on Old Torhtmund's *tún*. Spread out a little more so you don't hit each other. You've got to watch for the rats that come out, but don't forget where everyone is. Following a rat right into someone else's stick hurts like the torments of hell and it could cost you an eye."

The children were starting to get restless as we waited for something to happen. The *ceorl* finished mucking the stalls and left the stable smiling to see the children arrayed with their switches. After a little while there was commotion inside the barn — the cow mooing, the horses nickering, and the ordinarily placid oxen lowing and moving in their stalls. Young Torhtmund leaped through the door with his rune-stave drawn back, and I was a step behind him. The ferret was darting through the legs of an ox close behind a rat, and my son drew back his switch, and I only caught his arm in time to prevent him from learning first-hand what happens when you hit three quarters of a ton of nervous ox in a confined space. We'd be lucky if only the ferret was stomped to jelly.

The rat broke through the door, scrambling to my left, and we heard the noise of two switches striking the ground in rapid succession — snap — snap — and then the delighted shrieks from the girls announcing that they'd killed the rat. I looked outside and they were dancing around a twitching rat corpse about the size of my foot.

"Shite!" Young Torhtmund said, feeling done out of his first rat, and by his two sisters — a bitter potion to choke down.

"Don't worry, there's plenty more rats," I said.

I turned around and saw a man I didn't know watching us. He was standing at the door of the feed room, where there were barrels of grain and bales of hay. He was a little taller than me and younger by five or six winters. He had the thick shoulders and chest of a man who did a lot of heavy lifting in the course of a day. His hands were rough and his arms were well-muscled and his belly was flat. He was holding a water bucket and he looked angry.

"Who are you?" he demanded.

"I'm Hring," I said. "And you are . . . ?"

He scrutinized me for a moment; his glance flickered to Young Torhtmund and back to me.

"See a resemblance?" I asked.

"No one told me you were coming back."

"And if they had, who would they have told?"

"What?"

"This is Frod," Young Torhtmund said. "He's the *tún-geréfa*.

"How do you know Sentwine?"

"I don't," he said.

"My father told me that Sentwine recommended you."

He shrugged. "I heard Sentwine was asking around for a *tún-geréfa* and my father's a *tún-geréfa*, so I know the job."

"How long have you been here?"

"Long enough to make it plain I want no playing in my stable."

"*My* stable," I reminded him.

Frod glanced around the stable. The ferret was nowhere to be seen, but the animals were nervous. It was either turn them all out into the paddock so we could do a proper job on the empty stable or quit for the day, and since I didn't have the equipment I needed, nets in particular, I decided to recover the ferret and leave emperor Frod to rule his empire without disturbance.

"We'll go practice somewhere else," I said.

Ordgar was waiting outside, admiring the dead rat that Mæthild was prodding with the end of the switch.

"I see you met Frod," he said.

"Charming man."

"Charming as a bee sting on your dick," my nephew grinned.

"Had your differences?"

"Not yet," he said.

He shrugged and glanced at the children, which I interpreted to mean that there was a story he'd rather tell me when we were alone, or rather have Eadgiþ tell me. I thought he'd been hinting at something last night when we walked around the *tún*, but I had other things on my mind. I picked the dead rat up by the tail. It was a big doe that weighed a pound or a little more, and she'd been living the good life on spilled grain; the hair around all twelve of her distended teats was nuzzled bald.

I carried her over to the foundation of the stable and whistled and brushed the doe across the mouth of the hole. In a little while the hob's masked face poked out, and he sank his needle teeth into the rat. I pulled the doe away and drew the ferret out of the hole so I could pick him up.

I blew gently into his face and whispered what a good boy he was, finding that nasty fat rat so quick, and then I slipped him back into the leather sack and handed the rat to Young Torhtmund.

"Take her over to the pigs for breakfast," I told him.

As he was walking away, swinging the dead rat by the tail in an overhead circle, I noticed activity at the gate. I shaded my eyes and recognized two of my brothers, Gosfrith and Tilhmund, riding between the buildings toward me. Gosfrith was leading a horse that had a big hog carcass strapped to a frame on its back.

"We heard you were home," Gosfrith called out.

"Staying long?" Tilhmund asked, dismounting.

The ploughman's little boy walked over and took the reins from them and led the horses to the corral beside the barn. I embraced my brothers.

"You look different," Gosfrith said, stepping back.

"Tramping round south of the Tamesis changes you," I said.

My brother Gosfrith is a swine lord. He grows pork for the kindred and for sale, an occupation that keeps his muscles strong and his general aroma richly porcine. He's six years older than me, taller and heavier, and he has the darker coloring that came from the Celts on our mother's side of the family. Keeping pigs is a fulltime occupation, especially an operation the size of his, and he's always working on the holding. I was honored he'd taken time off.

Although he was darker, he looked more like our father the older he got. They had the same general build and height. He wore his hair cut short, whereas Old Torhtmund wore his long and braided, and he was smooth-shaved where the old man was bearded, but I reckoned when I looked at my oldest brother I was looking at my father's face when he'd been the same age.

Tilhmund was only a year older than me, and his resemblance to old Torhtmund wasn't as pronounced, but it was still noticeable. Tilhmund was a smith, and he had the upper body of a man who spent a lot of time hammering iron. He was the strongest of my brothers, even stronger than Mæl, and when we got together for festivals and celebrations he invariably won any contest that demanded strength.

"What's the hog for?"

"I thought you might not have a dead hog," Gosfrith said. "It's for us to eat, what the fock do you think? Let's build a fire. It'll take hours to roast this porker."

"The rest of the family's coming later," Tilhmund said. "If we're to have any time together, we have to have a family feast before Mæl's wedding. The wedding feast will be too big, and Derehild's side of the kindred will be there." He grimaced. "Not to mention Æthelwaru's kindred, all po faced because they don't approve of the marriage. So you never know what might happen."

Derehild was our grandfather's second wife and widow, and there was bad blood between the two sides of the kindred, except for our half-uncle Whitgar, who was everyone's friend.

There was an outdoor hearth behind the long house, near the kitchen and the stone ovens, and we led the packhorse there and unloaded the panniers. The hog was as big as me and, even gutted, weighed a little more. We skinned it and then threaded it onto the long iron spit. While we did that Ordgar raked the cold ashes out of the pit and built a structure of logs and charcoal and got a fire going. It would take an hour to blaze up and then burn down to a bed of cooking coals. The charcoal would burn hotter and accelerate the ignition of the logs. We used a few cartloads of seasoned oak that the fire would reduce to a blue-red bed of coals. When the blaze subsided, we mounted the spitted hog over the fire and organized the roster of men and boys who'd spend the next seven or eight hours turning it slowly in the heat.

While we worked, the routine daily activity of the *tún* went on around us. The shepherds sheared sheep in the wool barn, a girl milked the cows, and when she was finished, her little brother turned them out into the ten acre pasture with the rest of the herd, other women fed the hogs, geese, and chickens. Some of the *ceorls* had lived and worked on the *tún* before Oswith died, and we exchanged greetings. I was glad to see familiar faces.

I met one of the new families of *ceorls*, a ploughman called Cenhart and his wife Eohild and their two children. I liked that there were more children living on the *tún*. Brothers and sisters get tired of one another's company.

When Oswith was alive the hidage had supported twelve families of *ceorls*: four plowmen, three herdsmen, a bee keeper, an orchard man, a cook, a woodsman and a collier and their families had all taken my salt. There were even a few voluntary *theows* because of hard winters. When I disappeared into Northumbria, Old Torhtmund had closed up the *tún* and taken the children to live in his house, and half of the *ceorls* had left. Now at least one of the shepherds and the herdsman were back. The rest would return when we restored the stock.

"What do you make of Frod?" Gosfrith asked.

"I just met him this morning," I said.

"Ordgar says he's a wanker."

"Ordgar has a strong opinion, but I haven't heard the details."

Tilhmund stepped back when we had the hog in place over the flames and looked at it with approval. We all knew how to build a cooking fire, but Tilhmund was a smith and he knew the science of forge fires, so he was able to judge the heat of a fire from the color of the flames and coals and he knew how to adjust it with different fuels. His fires were things of beauty.

"Ordgar," I called out as he walked emerged from the long house. "Find us a barrel of beer or cider or something that will loosen our tongues so we can sit and gossip about everyone who isn't here to call us liars."

Ordgar turned his steps toward one of the sunken storehouses where several barrows leaned against the wall. There were a couple of rough tables near the kitchen that the cook used for preparing meals and we walked over and pulled out the benches and sat down to wait in the shade. The heat of the fire shimmered around the hog and fat started dripping into the flames.

Eadgiþ walked out of the long house and came over to join us. She was carrying a basket full of horn cups.

"I don't remember asking for cups," Gosfrith said.

"You're old and forgetful," she told him.

At thirty four, Gosfrith was 16 years older than Eadgiþ, and she seemed pleased to remind him of his advanced age. She sat down at the end of the bench and distributed the cups.

By mid-afternoon most of the rest of my family had arrived in waggons and on horseback and the *tún* had become a confusion of squealing and squabbling children playing in the shade of the tall elm trees. My brother Godfred and his wife Winfrith, my sister Elfilda and her husband Unlaf, my sister Enflæda (alone because her husband Scenwulf was delivering a team of oxen to someone in the neighboring hundred), and Gosfrith and Tilhmund's wives, Estrið and Godwyna, had all arrived and settled in around the tables to gossip and watch the hog roast, and we were opening the second barrel of beer. I felt like I was finally home.

Eadgiþ

I was the youngest in the household. The youngest always has trouble, or maybe everyone has their own different trouble because of where they fall in the order of things. When I was little, my sister Elfilda once told me, when she was angry because of something I'd done, that Flæd and Torhtmund only had me to replace Hring, who'd gone to the minster in Eoforwic. I've never forgotten that bit of childish hurtfulness, and even though I never believed it, I was always afraid that it *might* be true, though Flæd and Torhtmund treated me like they treated all my brothers and sisters. Who's to say what's in people's hearts? They did give Hring to the Church.

When Hring came back from Eoforwic I was only eight winters old, and I don't remember meeting him. What I remember is something from later. He was sitting alone in the long house after everyone else had gone to sleep, and I woke up because I had to pee. When I came back from the bucket I saw him sitting at the end of the hearth, poking at the fire with an iron rod to keep a small flame going.

I went over to where he was sitting and he made room for me on the bench and I climbed up beside him and he put his arm around me and we sat there for a long time not saying anything. Everyone else had known him before he'd gone to Eoforwic, and they all had stories about him, so I had a child's idea of who he was based on fragments of other people's misremembered events that had happened winters before I was born.

But I've always felt like I began to know him for myself that time we sat together on the bench by the hearth fire listening to the flames snap and flicker while everyone else was sleeping. When we finally talked, I don't even remember what we said. It was little enough, in any event. We were both strangers, but we were brother and sister, and it felt right for him to be there and for me to be there with him.

So I watched Hring with his children the night he came home for Mæl's wedding, and I thought of that other time, when I'd been about the age Mæthild was now. And now I watched Hring with our brothers and sisters while the hog roasted and we relieved one another turning the spit while the skin split and darkened into reddish brown in the heat and the fat dripped and hissed into the flames and the meat roasted.

We had the Church in common now, and leaving the Church, although he hadn't wanted to leave and I had. Because of that, I felt closer to him than I felt to the others. We could both read, and even though I was educated only enough to understand just how educated Hring had become in Eoforwic, having any education at all set me apart from everyone else I knew except him, and I'd begun to understand, in the little while I'd been home, what it must have been like for Hring to come back from the minster with his head full of languages and mathematics and philosophy and history to a family that distrusted what they didn't know and anyone who knew it. I don't think anyone else in the household understood. To them he was still mysterious after all these years.

I reckon that last summer, when he thought he was home for good, he must have thought he finally had his chance to be a member of the family and to raise his children in the kindred, but that chance had been snatched away before he'd even closed his fingers around it.

Hring was drinking and laughing while my brothers and sisters argued about whether it made more sense for Mæl and Æthelwaru to live in the house Mæl lived now or to build a bigger house to accommodate their future children. Then he caught my eye and smiled and came over to where I was sitting on the edge of the group.

"What's the story with Frod?" he asked.

My brother was always a surprise—he'd been back less than a full day and he already knew there was a story with Frod.

"Did Ordgar say something to you?"

"Ordgar told me Frod likes things his own way."

"He seems a competent *tún-geréfa*," I said, answering a question he hadn't asked.

Hring frowned and sipped from his cup.

"What else does he seem?" he asked.

"He seems to think he's entitled to have things as he likes them because he's the *tún-geréfa*."

Hring nodded but he didn't say anything. He just looked at me as if he were waiting for me to finish a thought.

"He watches me," I said after a pause. "Whenever he's around he's watching me. If I look at him, he's already looking at me. It makes my skin crawl. I'm one of the things he likes and he seems to think he's entitled to me as well."

Frod had been going about his business on the *tún* while we sat there drinking and talking and waiting for the hog to roast. Wherever he went in the *tún* I could see him stealing glances at us, not quite resentful, but as if we were *thegns* who were content to let the *ceorls* do the work. At least that's how it seemed. He'd been around long enough to know better than that. At least it was better than when I was there alone, what I could see in his looks then made me want to take a bath.

I'd joined the convent after an unhappy connection with a son of the *ealdorman's* horse *thegn* who'd been more interested in taking me into the hay mow than marrying me. Luckily, I broke it off before either happened, and then I put myself out of the reach of all young men with stiff pricks by taking vows.

Hring and Oswith had tried to talk me out of it. Hring said he'd seen men in Eoforwic who undertook the religious life for the wrong reasons and it had never turned out well. There was one of them in our own extended kindred, if I doubted the point he was making. But once I'd decided to take the veil, there was no turning back. I tried to live up to my vows, and I succeeded until I found myself under the authority of a stupid, incompetent, bitch. Hring had the same experience himself and reacted the same way. It's a family trait.

"Has he made advances?" Hring's eyes scanned the *tún* as if he were looking for Frod.

"If he did, it would be in the open; now it's like being spied on."

"It's easily gotten in the open if you want," Hring said. "I can have him on his way in ten minutes."

I shook my head and smiled. "It's good to have brothers to take care of you," I said. "But if you let them, you never learn to take care of yourself. Enflæda didn't get to be Enflæda because you took care of her; she got to be Enflæda because she wouldn't let you."

"So what do you want to do?"

"I'll take care of it after Mæl's wedding. We'll be busy enough until then without losing a *tún-geréfa* who knows his work."

"If that's what you want." Hring closed his eyes for a moment. "Thank you for living here. It's good for the children to live where their father and mother were happy. There's a favor I'd like to ask. Would you teach the children to read and write?"

"I can do that," I said.

"I'll arrange to get you the materials before I leave," he said.

Hring

It had been a long time since I'd been with my whole family for a meal, and I'd drunk enough that I was starting to feel low, missing Oswith and wishing that she was with me to enjoy the day. Everyone had liked Oswith. I used to think it was because getting married had given my family a definition of Hring that they could recognize and understand—husband and father. But everyone had loved Oswith for herself more than for anything having to do with me, and it was only wishful vanity that made me think otherwise.

Ordgar, who was turning into the master archer of the kindred, set up a straw butt and the older children were shooting arrows at it from a distance of the 10 long paces that Engelhard, Gosfrith's oldest son, had walked off while Ordgar established the shooting order. Arrows were flying thick and fast, several of them were even embedded in the targets.

"Uh, oh," Gosfrith said. "Brace yourselves." He nodded in the direction of the gate and we turned to see Mæl riding into the *tún*.

Mæl was late because it was a milling day; he'd been grinding flour since sunup. Apparently he'd packed the last of his customers and their bruised egos off his hidage and swept up the milling floor and come to join the feast. He dismounted at the stable door and tied his horse to the rail. He stretched, spread his ass cheeks with his left hand, and lifted his left leg slightly to release an unmistakable fart, too far away to hear or smell, and then started walking toward us. I stood up and went to meet him. There was a fine dust of brown flour in his hair.

"So it's finally happening," I said, hugging him.

I was lifted off the ground and spun around — Mæl being playful and happy to see me.

"Focking late as usual," he said.

"I'm a week early," I pointed out.

"You should've come a week before this," he said. "We could've had a good time drinking and fishing in the mill pond."

Fishing with Mæl was something I'd done when I was very young, before I'd gone to Eoforwic. For some reason, I was Mæl's favorite brother. Possibly because I'd been gone for ten winters and he hadn't had an opportunity to form the same bad opinions about me as an adult that he'd formed about the rest of my brothers, or possibly

112

because he was just a contrarian by nature. It didn't make him any less quick to point out my deficiencies as he saw them, or reluctant to explain what I ought to be doing in any given instance instead of whatever I *was* doing, but he'd had an inexplicable fondness for me ever since we were boys. I remember looking up to him, even though he was only four winters older. Age differences matter at the beginning and the end of life, but during the long middle they often don't seem so important.

And in the absence of children of his own, he'd taken it upon himself to become a presence in the lives of my children while I was in Northumbria, spending as much time as he could spare from the mill to be with them, playing and making himself agreeable in a way that he'd never bothered to attempt with his own brothers and sisters, except me. As a result, my children smothered him with a baffling and uncritical affection. Mæl was no different than anyone—he had love to share, and he needed love in return.

"Mæl," Osgiva shrieked when she saw him, running across the open ground into his embrace.

He scooped her up and threw her high into the air through the cloud of her giggles, catching her and tucking her under his right arm in the same motion as he extended his left arm to collect her sister, the normally reserved Mæthild. I smiled and stepped out of the way, a little jealous of how unreservedly happy they were to see him. I glanced back at the table where my brothers and sisters were shaking their heads, once more reminded that for a man given to profane bluster and gruff, lacerating opinion when he was dealing with adults, Mæl was also a man capable of surprising tenderness with children.

"Where's Æthelwaru?" I asked as he put her down.

"On her father's hidage, I reckon," he said. "The fat fock's keeping her there until the wedding. I haven't seen her for five or six months."

"He *is* a fat fock," my six year old daughter Osgiva agreed with conviction. While I'd been gone she'd apparently become the star pupil in Mæl's school of blunt, plain-spoken rhetoric. Æthelwaru's father might reasonably be characterized as a fat fock, but I could see no good end to my younger daughter embracing her uncle Mæl's unfiltered and reckless freedom of expression. It would certainly have a deleterious impact on her marriage prospects when she got older.

"We shouldn't point that out when he's close enough to hear," I said.

She looked at me as if I were an elf-shot moron. "Why would I do *that*?" she asked.

Mæl scooted my daughters on their way and stood up, surveying the cups on the table. "I'm thirsty," he said.

When Mæl's initial thirst was seen to, we sat together and talked companionably about his upcoming wedding.

"It took you long enough to agree on a date," I said.

"That fat fock wouldn't give his permission."

"What changed his mind?"

Mæl smiled. "Nothing. Little Bunny outfoxed him."

"How?"

"Even though he acts like it, her father isn't the head of the kindred. Her grandfather is. But he's got the old people's craziness, the kind that comes and goes. Still, Little Bunny goes to see him every day, and no one else does. So she waited until he wasn't crazy and then told him she wanted to wed and that her father wouldn't let her. Then she took old Wulfnoth to her father's *tún* straightaway before he could forget, and the old man called his sons together and told them how it was. Wulfnoth got his iron the same day as Old Torhtmund, and he wants the kindreds to join. Nothing Little Bunny's old Da could do to stop it after that."

"Well, congratulations, however it was managed."

"I was wondering if I could use the bath house," he said. "I suppose I ought to bathe for the wedding. Little Bunny likes it."

"Of course," I said, looking him over. "Maybe you'd like a bath before the real bath, you know, just to remember how it feels and get in practice."

"I remember how it feels," he said. "It's only been six weeks."

"I was going to fill the tub today and soak off

the ride from Cantwarabyrig," I said. "Shave this beard so people can recognize me."

"Doesn't look like you'll get to it now," he grinned, gesturing to our partying family. "I want your advice on the morning gift."

The *morgen-gifu* is the gift that the husband gives to the bride the morning after they consummate the marriage. The morning gift is an irrevocable settlement sufficient to see her through widowhood—hidage, livestock, coin, or all three. Since the bride wouldn't inherit in the event of her husband's death unless she'd born a living son, the morning gift was her insurance. The nature of the morning gift is defined exactly in the marriage contract, so I didn't understand what there was to advise him about.

"The morning gift isn't detailed in the wedding contract?"

"Not *that* morning gift," he said. "That morning gift's five hides of land. I mean something special, just for her. You and Oswith were always giving each another gifts, so I thought you might have some ideas. I was thinking of a long *seax*. What do you think?"

I suppose that for some men nothing says 'I love you' like twenty-four inches of pattern-welded iron under a thin sheen of oil, but to my mind a long *seax* lacked that personal touch women seem to treasure in an intimate gift. Unless Æthelwaru was thinking of turning out for *fyrd* duty, I doubted that a long *seax* would fill a need.

Still, I wasn't familiar with the contours of their intimacy, and for all I knew a long *seax* might be just the tangible expression of endearment that would moisten Æthelwaru's loins and unlock her knees. Despite her dimpled cheeks and winsome smile, she didn't seem the silk undergarment type. The great majority of the hours I'd spent in her company had been riding toward, committing, and riding away from horrific episodes of ghastly violence that demanded a certain familiarity with edged weapons. What did I know?

"Has she said she wants a long *seax*?"

"Not in so many words."

"Then what makes you think she'd like one?"

"When we were in Northumbria, she said it was easier to cut off a man's head with a *seax* than with an axe."

"That sounds more like an observation than a hint," I said. This was the sort of conversation you could unexpectedly find yourself involved in with Mæl and one of the reasons why some people found him offputting.

"Oswith always liked it when I gave her amber," I said.

Oswith had loved amber. The cloak pin she'd given me as a gift when we married had a large amber head with a bee trapped in it. Her father was a beekeeper, and she said that I was as industrious as a bee, so it had been a meaningful gift.

"Amber," he said thoughtfully as he sipped his beer.

Old Torhtmund and Flæd arrived just before it was time to eat. Old Torhtmund had left his new *tún-geréfas* to sort out the guests. His old *geréfas* had been killed a year ago — one because he'd been mistaken for me and the other because he'd turned right instead of left when we went after the man who'd killed his friend.

My homecoming lasted all the long evening and into the night. We set up two other tables, so there was room for everyone to eat without digging their elbows into their neighbor's ribs, and the families of the *ceorls* who lived on the *tún* came out to help us eat the hog. Mæl counseled them about problems they were unaware they had and offered his opinions on tending sheep, wrighting iron, ploughing fields, and keeping bees for their benefit. We opened another barrel of beer and ate the meal that the cook had prepared while my brothers and sisters and I sat in the shade drinking. I soon discovered that despite my being gone a year almost nothing had changed. The two biggest differences were that, at long last, Mæl would marry and that my youngest sister had returned from the convent.

When Mæl was off having a piss, I drew my younger brother Godfred aside for a word about the morning gift conversation. I had an idea, but I wanted to surprise Mæl, and I needed someone to ride up to Eoforwic to visit my Frisian merchant friends, who'd been invited to the wedding.

"They're not hard to find," I told him. "Anyone on Fossbank can take you to Gisl. I'll give you a letter introducing you and telling him what I want. If you leave early you can be back the same day, or you can stay overnight and Rud will show you the sights — my treat. Ever been to Eoforwic?"

"Once," he said. "It's a big, stinking place with a lot of stone buildings."

"It is that," I agreed. "But Mæl's taken a special interest in the children while I've been gone, and I want to do this for him."

"Did he ask you to get him something particular?"

I shook my head.

"Then whatever you get won't be right. You know that, don't you?"

"I'll take the chance."

Godfred was a year younger than me and his wife was four years younger than he was. Together they'd produced four daughters. He lived in a house of women who doted on him and whom he loved, but I thought he might like an opportunity to have some time away from all that doting.

"Alright," he agreed. "I'll go the day after tomorrow."

My new *tún-geréfa*, Frod, made a brief appearance to fill a plate, but he took his food off into the darkness somewhere, as if the presence of my family was disrupting his evening routine.

"Does anyone else think it's strange to avoid

the man whose *tún* you manage?"

"A good beating might teach the insulting ass-wipe something" Mæl said.

This seemed a reasonable solution to my brother, who's more sensitive to perceived insolence or disrespect directed at his kindred than he is to any directed at himself. Mæl has the thick skin of an old ox, but a finely-honed sense of family honor. It's another of his charming contradictions because he dispenses offhand discourtesy like an almoner handing out day-old bread to beggars, although he'd be genuinely surprised if you called his attention to it. Ironically, last summer Mæl had been thoroughly beaten and had learned nothing from the experience.

I knew this because he'd confided to me that it was Æthelwaru's brothers who'd beaten him in an attempt to discourage his attentions to their sister. He'd sworn me to secrecy about it. "No use causing more trouble," he said. It had taken me a long time to realize that I hadn't imagined the exchange, so incomprehensibly reasonable and un-Mæl-like a sentiment it was.

"Perhaps not the best approach to take," Old Torhtmund said.

"It's just his way," Gosfrith said. "He's still figuring out his position. Would *you* be a *tún-geréfa* for anyone in this family?"

"Well, he's *your tún-geréfa*," Mæl acknowledged with a shrug. After all these years of having his most reasonable solutions and advice ignored

by everyone in his family without the nous to recognize their merit, he'd grown philosophical
about it.

When we'd eaten our fill, we cut up the remainder of the hog and packed it into baskets and
put them in the spring house where the cool air
would keep the pork for a day or so. The *ceorls* returned to their houses to rest for tomorrow's
work, and we built up the fire again and sat beside
the blazing logs and I told my family about my
year on the road. Offa had kept his word and there
was no greater Mercian presence in Elmet than
there had been before I left, and my kindred was
grateful. Neither had the Northumbrian *thegn* who
thought I'd killed his son renewed the violence
against my family. The Mercians had made that
incipient feud disappear, as I'd been promised, in
exchange for my service. But my family didn't let
their gratitude get in the way of their utilitarian
practicality. When they learned I had a trained ferret with me, they made me promise to visit each of
the *túns* and kill as many rats as I could.

Individually, or in pairs, we visited Oswith's
grave during the evening, as if everyone had quietly remarked her absence and wanted to have a
private moment with her. Because her husband
Scenwulf was on the road delivering a couple of
yoke of oxen, Enflæda and I made the walk to the
cemetery together after dark.

We paused at the entrance to the walled enclosure, listening to the family's loud conversation

come through the darkness as everyone talked over everyone else—laughing, interrupting, arguing, insisting, and demanding attention. The edges of the long house were outlined in red by the firelight, and sparks rose up into the trees with the smoke and heat, tracing swift, erratic trails before they burned out. We could hear the crackle of the flames and smell the smoke and the roast pork.

"She's lying here listening to us," Enflæda said as my brother Tilhmund's laughter echoed away under the elms.

"They can hear us all the way in Loidis," I assured her.

"We haven't been all together since you left," she said as we walked up the slope toward the stone cross where Oswith was buried.

I thought about that last gathering, before I'd gone off with Bynna.

"I had a little brother once," Enflæda said. "He was a funny little boy who liked to pretend he was a bird swooping low over the home field with his arms out like wings. Do you remember him?"

I did remember him, but it was a fragmentary memory I had to reassemble like the pieces of a dropped pot. I'd liked to play the bird game when I was little, but after I went to Eoforwic I'd stopped.

"He went away north when he was small," I said.

"He wasn't the same when he came back," Enflæda said.

"No, he wasn't." The man who came back to Elmet was different than the boy who went north to Eoforwic. It was hard even to see the ghost of the boy who liked to pretend he was a bird. "He was lost when he came home."

"I know. I wasn't sure you'd ever find your way back."

"I wasn't either. Oswith brought me home."

"Then you changed into someone else."

"I changed into a better person."

"Maybe. Different, anyway."

"I changed into someone who belonged."

"Belonged here. After you came back you still thought you belonged in the minster."

"I had to unlearn the one to learn the other."

"And you belonged to Oswith and the children and to Sentwine's *hird* and the Law, but you've never quite belonged to the kindred."

"The kindred gave me up."

"And the kindred took you back."

"That's as may be. But when you're given up it's hard to trust they mean it when they take you back. You're always waiting to be given up again."

We were late getting up the next morning. Old Torhtmund and Flæd had gone home, a little more than a mile across the hidage, but my brothers and sisters lived farther afield and had stayed what was left of the night. When it clouded up and started to rain, we moved inside and put all the children to bed on the sleeping platform, covered them with blankets and fleeces and left them in a pile on the mattress of fresh-cut meadow grass for mutual warmth, and then we gathered around the hearth to drink and gossip, and we'd all fallen asleep where we were when sleep claimed us.

The cook moving around preparing breakfast, and the smell of fresh bread woke us to a damp, cloudy morning. The rain had stopped in the night, and while we broke our fast we determined the order in which I'd visit their *tún*s with the ferret. Mæl and Gosfrith were the most plagued by the vermin because rats love a mill and a hog farm above almost all other things, so I agreed to sort them first.

The children insisted that they accompany me, which meant that I had to spend the rest of the day teaching them not to hit each other with the sticks or kill the ferret in their excitement. Ordgar fetched the nets and my gear from Old Torhtmund's *tún,* and we moved the animals out of the stable and located all the holes in the foundations. I showed them how to secure the nets and spread them over the openings and then we let the ferret into the tunnels and stood back to wait for whatever bolted.

I divided the available holes among the children and was glad to see that they were spread out enough that my helpers weren't a danger to each other.

"Now you've got to pay attention because you never know when a rat will get into a net. As soon as one's caught, kill it quick. Make sure it's dead before you take it out of the net. A rat bite's a nasty, festering thing."

Ordgar was covering the back side of the stable. He was a dab hand with a bow, and it was a good opportunity for him to practice snap shots. I put the girls inside the stable and the boys on opposite sides and I covered the front. To keep them interested I told them that whoever killed the most rats would get a penny. After a slow start, the ferret located the nest and rats started breaking for open space all along the foundations.

An hour later I was paying Young Torhtmund a penny while his brother and sisters looked envious. He overcame his initial humiliation when his sisters killed the first rat and rallied to kill seven rats of his own; the rest of the children killed nine between them. Ordgar had shot five more. No one had been injured, and the ferret was dancing the happy ferret dance in the dirt and singing '*dook, dook, dook,*" which had surprised the children until Gulhere started dancing with it and they all started dancing and Ordgar was laughing so hard he had trouble unstringing his bow.

"All right," I said. "You're trained. Let's clean up this mess. Feed the ferret and throw the rats in the hog pen. We leave early in the morning for Mæl's *tún.*"

Mæl

It was a good day to kill rats, a little cloudy and cool, though I've never seen a bad day for killing rats, focking vermin. They came early in the day, Ordgar driving a waggon with the children in back and Hring riding some bad-tempered horse from the south that had crazy eyes. I could see from its gait that it was only waiting for an opportunity to cause trouble, and Hring isn't a great horseman.

"Where'd you get that horse?" I asked him.

"In Cantwarabyrig," he said. "His name's *Steðefæst*."

I had a laugh at that. One look and I could see it was the horse had an evil set of mind, and there was nothing reliable about it.

"Got a hard mouth, dunnit?" The horse and I sized each other up. It rolled those crazy eyes when it looked at me, like it was planning to nip me if I got too close. If it did, I'd have to give it a hard punch in its muzzle. Sometimes that worked; sometimes not—made me feel better, though.

"He's a hire horse. Had a lot of riders. Picked up bad habits."

Hring always tried to see the other side of things, but I didn't give a fock if the horse had a hard life and had been rented out to arseholes in the past. I didn't want it to throw my brother. It wasn't Hring's fault the horse was proud-cut and its life wasn't all fresh oats and mares in season.

"Well, get down and we'll put it in the stable. There's no time to cure it of its bad habits today."

The children jumped out of the waggon and came over to hug me. I threw them up into the air and caught them one at a time, oldest to youngest.

"What's this?" I asked. "You all ratcatchers now?"

"Father taught us yesterday," Osgiva said. "Torhtmund made a penny."

"Made a penny, did you?" I asked him. He looked proud of himself. "How many did you get?"

"Seven." Pride ran off him like water after a walk in the rain, as if he'd killed seven Mercians in the shield wall.

"I reckon we should set the same stakes," I told them. "Whoever kills the most rats gets a penny."

They scampered back to the waggon to get their nets and willow wands. Ordgar had his yew bow, like always. My nephew can shoot the eyes out of a sparrow at fifty yards with his yew bow.

"There's a lot of rats down on the wheel house floor," I said. "Shite, there are a lot everywhere. It's a mill."

"Don't the cats keep them down?" Hring asked.

"Can't keep up with them," I said. I had a lot of cats, nine at the moment, cats come and go, and they kept the mice down and killed some of the smaller rats, but rats breed faster than cats eat. The Dog Man kept trying to talk me into one of those little rat dogs that'll kill rats until it runs out of rats, but I don't like dogs much — they take up too much of your time.

The children came back with the nets, and we went into the mill. There were cracks in the joinery and the wattle where the rats came onto the grist floor at night.

"Put the nets over those holes," Hring said, pointing them out. Gulhere and Torhtmund started to secure the nets.

I turned around and the two girls were standing behind me like a couple of little abbesses waiting for the second coming of Christ, looking all sorrowful and grave. Osgiva was holding a bundle of willow wands and Mæthild was holding the ferret, stroking it between the ears.

"We have to teach you about the ferret," Osgiva said.

"What about the ferret, little princess?" I asked her.

"You have to be careful not to hit the ferret

when you swing at a rat."

"Won't the rats get caught in the nets?"

"Most of them," Osgiva said. "But if one gets out and runs and the ferret's behind it you have to be careful."

"Because if you hit the ferret," Mæthild said, "you'll crush it like a tick."

"I promise I'll be careful," I said.

"Because you're really, really big," Osgiva explained patiently. "And if you kill the ferret, we won't be able to kill more rats."

"I understand, little princess," I said. "I really do."

I saw Hring standing behind them smiling.

"Here's a stick," Mæthild said. "We should practice before we turn the ferret loose."

Mæthild and Osgiva taught me how to work the ferret while the boys set out the nets. Hring and Ordgar walked all over the mill. Hring kept getting down on his hands and knees to see how things looked to the rats.

"If you use your bow you'll hit one of us," I told Ordgar. "There's the pond on one side of the mill and too much machinery down by the wheel. And the millrace is on one side and the spillway is on the other. Better take a wand."

So Ordgar unstrung his bow and put it in the waggon.

"What have you got to drink?" Hring asked.

"I have a good sweet well," I told him and we went outside to get some water before we started while the boys set the nets and the girls made a fuss over the ferret, telling it about all the rats that were waiting.

"How's Æthelwaru?" he asked.

"I truly haven't seen her in months," I told him. "The *mæsse-thegn* confesses her every week and brings me messages."

"But he says she's well?"

"She's as well as a girl eager to be off her father's *tún* can be."

I dipped a fresh bucket of water, and we both had a long drink. It was cool and sweet like I told him it was.

"Any more trouble from her brothers?"

"No," I said.

Back in the mill, the boys had all the nets set, and the girls had the ferret on its lead sniffing at the holes in the wall, and Ordgar was back from the waggon. He was looking at all my river stones set on the wall beams. There was a film of light brown milling dust over all of them.

"Any new stones?" Ordgar asked.

"None lately," I said. Some people thought I was crazy to have all those smooth river stones, but I told them they were handy to throw at rats if I saw any. If the ferret was any good I wouldn't be throwing that many stones for a while. Ordgar took a few staves from the bundle and went outside to watch along the foundation that faced the house, and Hring nodded at Mæthild and went outside to get into position along the foundation by the millrace. I went outside and stood by the spillway. The race and the spillway were almost dry because I'd closed the sluice gate that morning and the outflow of the pond was diverted around the mill. There was a narrow path between the foundation and the water on the pond side of the mill, but there was no room for anyone to stand there and swing a stick. I'd like to have whistled up some of the cats to wait along that foundation but you can't tell cats anything, so I didn't bother.

Young Torhtmund and Gulhere went downstairs into the wheel room.

"Now?" Mæthild called out from the milling floor.

"Now," Hring called back.

Hring

e killed 35 rats at the mill, which put Mæl in such a good mood that he actually laughed in a way that wasn't frightening to see.

Watching him with the children made me think that he'd be a good father to his own. Still, a father's expectations of his children are often different from their uncle's, and unexpected attitudes based on a different kind of responsibility often emerge when a man's dealing with his own offspring, so in the end I decided to reserve judgment on Mæl's parental potential. All that I cared about was how he acted with my children, and I have to admit that in some ways he was better with them than I was.

The girls killed 16 rats on the milling floor and they couldn't agree on who killed how many, both of the girls hitting some of them at the same time, so in the end Mæl gave them each a penny because the boys had only killed nine in the wheel room. Between us, Mæl, Ordgar, and I killed another 15. Mæl was happy as a hog in mud when the boys piled all the rats in the yard for his inspection. His hogs seemed even happier than Mæl when we dumped the rats into their pen and they started to gobble them up. Torhtmund was down at the mouth because he'd been eclipsed by his sisters.

We spent a day on each of my brothers' and sisters' *túns*. When some of the cousins wanted to help (mostly because of the ferret), the children took time to teach them the dos and don'ts of ferreting. My children were protective of the ferret and one another. Ordgar assumed direct supervisory authority and, where manpower allowed, I used the time to catch up individually with my brothers and sisters.

They all had overlapping stories to tell me of the past year—births and deaths; sowings, growings, and harvestings; and, disturbingly if not surprisingly, rumblings of discontent from some of Derehild's line. It seemed that Derehild was taking advantage of Eadgiþ leaving the convent to stir up trouble, as she'd done when I'd expelled from the minster in Eoforwic.

Derehild was a sour old apple, withered in her years and—in her hatred of Old Torhtmund—she was without equal. My aunt Godgyth's death, long before any of us were born, remained a raw sore for Torhtmund and his brothers and sisters, and it set the tone for all relations with their *stéop-móðor*. And for her part, Derehild knew where all the raw spots were and she never hesitated to rub them with salt when it suited her.

First there were rumors that Eadgiþ had been expelled for unnatural acts with another nun. Those rumors abruptly stopped when Gosfrith, looking into a drinking establishment in Loidis for a quick one at the end of a long day at the swine market, overheard one of Derehild's grandsons laughing about Eadgiþ's supposed perversions. My brother announced his displeasure by introducing a wooden stool to the side of his cousin's head with great speed and precision. They had to pour a bucket of water on the cousin to wake him up. Then Gosfrith told him he was looking at an appeal for slander at the *gemót* unless he retracted said slander on the spot.

Then they started to hear rumors of Eadgiþ practicing her unnatural acts on my children. Tilhmund was reluctant to tell me about that rumor, not because he thought I might believe it, but because he thought I might hunt down whoever was spreading it and give him a Lullo-class beating, unnecessarily in the event, because that rumor had already been quashed in the usual way, this time by Mæl, and in a fashion that clearly demonstrated the official future reaction to its continued circulation. That Mæl had neglected to mention it could only mean that he considered the episode satisfactorily dealt with.

After that, they left off spreading calumnies about Eadgiþ and started back in on me, speculating that I was absent from the hundred because I was on another drinking binge and had abandoned my children again. My younger brother, Godfred, had taken that one directly to Creda, who went personally to Derehild's *tún* with the message that I was a *sundornotu-geréfa* performing extraordinary services for the *ealdorman* and for Offa, and that if my absence became a matter of common gossip that called unnecessary attention to that service and put its outcome in jeopardy, there would be grave consequences involving Mercian killing *thegns*. Derehild might be a bilious old bitch, but she was smart enough to know that Creda was serious, and all rumors concerning me dried up within a couple of days.

Having been dissuaded from slandering me or Eadgiþ, the speculation about Mæl and Æthelwaru began, slowly at first, barely distinguishable from the general complaints and stories about Mæl's disgruntlements that people routinely shared for their entertainment value. Mæl stories were common currency in the hundred. Fueled by Æthelwaru's close confinement to the family hidage, the rumor began to take shape that she was pregnant with Mæl's bastard and that family honor would demand an appeal at the *gemót* and possibly the breaking of the betrothal. Loose talk about Mæl planting a bastard in Æthelwaru's belly could jeopardize all of Creda's hard work finalizing the bride price and composing a satisfactory marriage contract. My family assumed that Æthelwaru's father was looking, even at this late date, for an excuse to subvert the marriage. If his daughter's honor was called publically into question, Æthelwaru's father would have to acknowledge it and possibly take it to Law. No one wanted that.

My sister Enflæda took it upon herself to confront her step-aunt Edu, mother of the drunken priest Lullo, in the market at Loidis about the disturbing increase in rancor that was gathering head prior to Mæl's wedding. Enflæda assured her that while, as kindred, they were all invited; they'd better be on their best behavior because if they caused any trouble Enflæda would personally set the dogs on them and laugh herself silly as the mutts harried them off the hidage. And in addition, if anything happened to preempt the wedding—say, disturbing rumors about the condition of the bride to be—and that preemption could be traced to Derehild's side of the kindred, the torments of Hell would be preferable to Mæl's expressions of disappointment. Just a friendly word of warning from one concerned woman to another.

So that had been the end of the talk about Mæl knocking up Æthelwaru, and since no one had seen Æthelwaru for five or six months while her father kept her sequestered on his *tún* during the final frenzy of the bride-price negotiations, there was no way to prove or disprove the allegation.

All that week, while the children and I killed rats for my brothers and sisters, the camp in Old Torhtmund's home field swelled with guests. Most of the time the gradual growth was unnoticeably slow; you woke up in the morning and there were a few more tents, and the edge of the encampment was a little farther from the pavilion in the center. But in addition to the unremarked appearance of new guests and their tents there were three great arrivals — three important entrances — although only one of them was consciously striving for the effect.

Sprot

The ride down from Eoforwic took two days. The Frisians had a couple of waggons to themselves, and a dozen armed men rode with us to discourage any wolf's heads who thought a Frisian merchant might make a good payday for their thieving. It was probably more Frisians than most people ever saw in one place unless they'd been to the trading *wic* in Eoforwic. Gisl and his son Radbod rode together in one of the waggon, but the other son, Rud, liked the mobility of a horse. I didn't blame him. Waggons are slow, even with a couple of mules in the traces.

The first day we got as far as the Wharfe River, and the old ferryman that Hring knew carried us across. It took him four trips, but he only took payment for three after Gisl told him we were going to the wedding of Hring's brother. He remembered Mæl from last summer when we rode north to Catræth to get Hring's son back. Hring's brother is hard to forget. He's a head taller than anyone else I've ever met and has big miller's shoulders and a shuffling walk.

Mæl isn't shy about telling you what he thinks, either. Most of Hring goes on in his head with his mouth shut, but most of his brother Mæl goes on out in the open, where everyone can see and hear it. At least that's what it looks like. Once or twice I wondered. When I'd gone to Elmet last summer, Hring's brothers mistook me for a killing *thegn* and beat me bloody because they thought I'd tried to kill Hring and killed his father's *tún-geréfas* instead, one by mistake and the other when I was trying to get away. Someone had just beaten Mæl as badly, and we were laid up together for a few days, so I got to hear all his theories and opinions. He was loud and angry, and he raged about what he'd do to the scum sucker who was trying to kill his little brother.

But when he was quiet I could see that things were going on behind his eyes; in his way, he was as much inside himself as his brother. When Hring's children were with him he was a different man altogether — as gentle then as he was blustery otherwise. I thought that he wanted everyone to think he was a loud, stupid miller like the ones in the stories because it saved him having to explain who he really was. The children were angry with Hring for leaving them on their grandfather's *tún* and walking back to Eoforwic and staying drunk that autumn and winter. Who could blame them? When they needed him, he was gone. But Mæl took his place, and when they were together I could see that they loved him for it.

And that woman of his. Christ on a galloping elephant but she's something. The first time I saw her she was naked and covered with blood, and there were bodies scattered all around, and she'd done for half of them herself. On the ride to Catræth she was as hard as any of the *geréfas,* and when we fought the killing *thegns* in Gladwin's hall she was as fierce as any man I ever stood with in the shield wall. None of us who were there will ever forget her fighting for Hring's oldest son, and she was the one who found the boy and did for the bitch that beat him before we got there.

She's a fine woman, if a little raw boned and rangy for my taste.

I was glad they were getting married.

My sister Somerild and her children were with me. She knew Hring a little, but she'd never met his brother. I told her all about him when I got back home last summer, after Hring went south with the *sundornotu-geréfa* who came to fetch him for Offa. When the message came about his wedding she insisted that we all go, children as well.

I think my sister fancies Hring, though he never seemed to think about her that way. In his head he's still married to his wife Oswith. I'd been in Elmet long enough to understand what she meant to everyone who knew her, and to see how everyone grieved for her. None of them so awful to watch as Hring, but none of them closer to her, either, except their children.

Somerild never believed he'd killed the *thegn's* son. She couldn't tell me why, but after she saw him the first time she said she just knew. Women have the luxury of trust and belief, but street *geréfas* have to dump trust and belief as soon as they can because they're too heavy to carry around. They'll slow you down with hesitation and get you killed.

We stayed in Tathaceaster the middle night and came the rest of the way the following day. There were already a lot of tents pitched in the home field outside Old Torhtmund's *tún,* and the wedding was still a few days away. I could see how they watched us when we rode through the gate. Frisians and Northumbrians, not the usual guests at an Elmetsætan wedding. But Hring was there when we arrived, and his father and mother greeted us with all the proper gestures of hospitality—bread and salt and water, and then a cup of mead.

Hring was glad to see us. We'd been five hours in the waggon and we had to stretch our legs when we got there, but Hring showed Gisl's men where he'd saved space for us inside the walls of the *tún,* and while they put up the tents and saw to the horses and mules we went inside and met Hring's mother and father.

Old Torhtmund seemed to have gotten over

his embarrassment about beating me last summer. He welcomed us as if we were long lost members of his kindred and apologized for not having more time to spend with us. Apparently, Old Torht-mund had been looking forward to talking to Gisl because he was going to cut a few acres of timber and he wanted to sell it in Eoforwic. Gisl was in-terested in acting as the middle man for a modest handling fee.

Hring showed us to a table in the hall where the beer barrel waited our attention and Somerild took the children to explore the *tún* and the camp in the home field, where we could hear the music and laughter of their pre-wedding roistering. Things were bustling as guests arrived. The rou-tine business of the *tún*, except for the essential tasks required to care for the animals, was aban-doned until after the wedding.

"Godfred said he delivered my letter," Hring said as we sat down.

"We tried to make him welcome," Radbod said. "But he refused our hospitality; said he had to get back home right away."

"He doesn't like the city," Hring said. "Too many people for him."

"To each as each prefers," Radbod shrugged. "As to the letter, our amber stock isn't the best at the moment, but I brought everything we have so you can take your pick. It's my gift for the wed-ding."

"I can't let you do that," Hring said.

"How are you going to stop me?"

"We've all brought wedding gifts," Rud told him.

Radbod was giving amber; Gisl was providing a bed frame that was massive enough to withstand at least the first month of Mæl and Æthelwaru's marriage; Somerild and I were giving them an embroidered weaving; well, Somerild did the work. Rud had his own idea of what made a good wedding gift.

Radbod sent for the amber chest, and when it arrived from the baggage waggon he unlocked it and displayed a selection of jewelry on the table — brooches, necklaces, earrings, pendants, rings — just about anything you could wish for. If this was their depleted stock, I could only imagine what a full inventory looked like. There were lots of things there that Juthwara would have liked, but I couldn't afford any of them. Hring sorted through the jewelry and set aside a gold necklace with two large amber pieces worked into symmetrical designs and a pair of earrings that matched.

"I brought Mæl a special present," Rud said. "Something to start conversations at the mill."

"My brother has no trouble starting conversations; all he has to do is express an opinion about the person he's talking to and conversation almost always follows. What special present might it be?"

"The kind that's a surprise," Rud said with a sly smile that should have made Hring worry.

I looked at Radbod, but he just shook his head.

Rædnoth

It was our off week between gemót sessions, and Sentwine's hird assembled in Loidis and rode to Old Torhtmund's *tún* as a group two days before the wedding. Even the scribes came. Jaruman was performing the ceremony. Most of us had met Hring's family over the years, but since we'd rendered service to the kindred by going into Northumbria with him to get his son Young Torhtmund, they made certain we were always welcome.

The guests who were tenting it out in the home field were encouraged to stay out of the enclosed *tún* by the *tún-geréfas* on the gate. Not that it mattered; there was plenty out there to entertain them. My *geréfas* and I are used to managing large crowds, and we could see right away that the two *tún-geréfas* were overmatched by the number of the wedding guests.

I had a word with Sentwine and then with the lads; we'd come to celebrate a wedding, not work, but they agreed that it was better to stop trouble before it started than after, so we proposed to Old Torhtmund that he let us sort some of the confusion in his home field. The problems created when a crowd of drunks attempts to get on with the activities of daily living, which, for drunks in large crowds mostly involves staying drunk and being conspicuously annoying while they do it, were well within our scope. So the two squads filled their cups and spread out through the encampment, each accompanied by one of Old Torhtmund's *tún-geréfas*, having a quiet word on the virtues of moderation wherever they thought such counsel was necessary, and where more forceful persuasion was required they demonstrated their authority with discretion.

While we were imposing some order on the revelers in the home field, the judiciary of Elmet gathered in Old Torhtmund's hall to drink and relax. Creda, the chief advocate to the *witangemót*, the priest Jaruman, and the advocates, Sentwine, Ingulf, and Cwichelm, gathered at a table and raised their cups with Old Torhtmund, toasting the future prosperity and happiness of his son Mæl, wishing him long life and many sons.

Jaruman was officiating at the wedding, and he absented himself from the drinking so he could go back to his tent to work on the sermon.

When the protocol of hospitality was satisfied

and Old Torhtmund had left us to greet other arriving guests, they reverted to talk about the *gemót* courts, which allowed us to avoid the dangerous ground of who might or might not be sleeping with whose wife. Cwichelm was suspected of being more attentive to Ingulf's much younger wife than was seemly when he'd been Ingulf's assistant. By the time Hring arrived, we were still sober and carefully avoiding provocative topics, but Ingulf and Cwichelm were sitting as far apart as possible and not addressing one another directly.

The third advocacy in Elmet had been Hring's for the taking, but when Oswith died he'd pissed that easy opportunity away. Ingulf put his assistant Cwichelm forward for the position, as much to remove him from the vicinity of his voluptuous young wife as to fill a vacancy that would coincidentally reduce his own workload and give him more time alone with his voluptuous young wife—a win-win outcome as far as Ingulf was concerned.

Ingulf kept his wife in the tent when he wasn't with her, and he made certain that when he wasn't with her he was within an arm's length of his former assistant Cwichelm. There was much discussion about whether Cwichelm was really the secret lover of Ingulf's wife, the bounteous Thryth. It was hard for the *geréfas* to believe that Cwichelm had been disguising his lustful impulses all those years, successfully convincing us, by his refusal to talk coarsely about women and his faraway eyes and his soft manner, that all his sexual attentions were probably directed at boys.

I never thought he was a pederast. I just thought he was bookish and soft spoken, but bored *geréfas* are like old women for gossip — in the absence of anything real to talk about, they happily invent something. Perhaps they just thought that it was funny to imagine willow-wristed Cwichelm having it off with old Ingulf's young wife right under his nose.

Ingulf was a prickly old buzzard who never hesitated to offload an unpleasant task on someone else, and we'd pulled additional duty over the years that everyone thought was rightly his, so making fun of him was just a bit of vindictive sport.

Ingulf wasn't a confrontational man, so he didn't go directly to either his wife or his assistant to discover the truth or falsity of the rumor when he finally heard it. Instead, he brooded and watched and did everything he could to be certain that they were never alone together. That's why he'd put his assistant forward for the third advocacy when Hring disappeared into Northumbria.

You'd think he'd relax after his assistant's promotion and forget about such an improbable and unproven slander, but not Ingulf. Ingulf was one of those insecure old worriers who become happily mired in their worry. He periodically gave his former assistant long speculative looks from under his bushy eyebrows and over the rim of his cup. He seemed to think this disguised his interest in Cwichelm, but had apparently not given much thought to the fact that in order to keep doing this he had to keep drinking. As a result he was quickly outpacing the rest of us in consumption.

After a while he closed his eyes and dozed off. Conversation continued, and then it was Cwichelm's turn to look at his former advocate. After it was clear that Ingulf was sleeping — the soft snoring was a clue — Cwichelm asked for directions to the cess pit and excused himself from the table. After he was gone, conversation lagged as we smiled at one another and Sentwine raised his eyebrows in an expression of confused inquiry. Creda shrugged. Hring finished his cup of beer and told us he had to go kill some rats. Possibly. Probably he just didn't want to be around when Ingulf woke up to discover that Cwichelm was gone.

The Priest Jaruman

how I miss living in **Abingdon.** I miss the monastic life of scholarship and prayer, the family of men and women devoted to the tranquility of worship and the contemplation of God, the quiet gardens, the cool, shadowed church, the smell of candle smoke and burning tallow on a cold morning in the dark quire.

I left Abingdon twenty-two winters ago and since then I've been back four times; I cried each time I left. We all have a home, and Abingdon is mine. I pursue my work as the *mæsse-thegn* for the advocate Sentwine's *hird*; I am their confessor and keeper of the instruments of the ordeal, but only as a penitential sacrifice in the service of the Law, because without the Law there is nothing. I've lived in Elmet for years, but my heart turns to Abingdon when I think of home.

The rough justice of the *gemót* courts is the tangible manifestation of the king's law, an approximation of the Law of God, an imperfect echo of its perfection. Sentwine is a good man doing the best he can do within the flawed structure of the king's *dóms*, and the *geréfas* are good men, and Hring is a good man.

I'm a lazy and imperfect man, and I miss Abingdon because faith was easy there, in a community of the faithful, but in Sentwine's *hird* faith is difficult. I give them the sacraments and listen to their confessional secrets and absolve them of their routine sins. I know who they are. The *geréfas* all have the type of uncritical and unexamined faith that doesn't withstand adversity, the type of weak, untried faith that can break under its first test, as dry and brittle as a dead pine branch. They believe because they've been told to believe, and because everyone around them believes.

That's why I went with them into Northumbria, so they would do only what was required to take back Hring's son and no more. The temptation to do more is always there when blood is spilled. I was unsuccessful.

I never thought that Hring's faith was as fragile as it proved to be when his wife died, and he crumbled like a structure made of drying sand. Perhaps her death was just the final blow, finishing what had begun years ago when his family gave him to the minster in oblation.

I could see a spiritual emptiness in Hring's eyes. Although he had never told me and still carried on as if he had faith, I knew that he didn't have faith in anything now except his children and those of us who had gone with him into Northumbria. His kindred had betrayed him to the Church, the Church had betrayed him to a life he was unprepared for, and his belief in the structure and permanence and necessity of the Law had betrayed him to the Mercians.

When I was younger, I thought that faith and belief were the same thing. I thought that they were both the residue of God's grace, and that you either have faith and believe or you don't, and that those who have faith are saved and those who don't are damned. Life has taught me that faith isn't that simple, which is why I think I miss Abingdon. Belief is based on evidence in reality; faith is belief without the evidence; belief is a subjective interpretation of things — faith is their conceptual acceptance. My confessor at Abingdon once told me that you can chose to believe, that in spite of the absence of convincing evidence in the present you can choose to believe in the convincing evidence of the past, or the promise of the future set down in divinely inspired scripture. He seemed to think that was the same as faith, and for a long time I did as well.

But after all these years I think there's a clear distinction between belief and faith. I've met too many true believers not to have observed it. Belief is the opposite of faith. Belief is the insistence that the truth is what a man wants it to be. Believers adhere to a truth that fits their subjective, preconceived ideas. Faith is an unreserved availability to a more objective truth, whatever it turns out to be. Faith is without precondition; it's a step into the darkness. Everyone has a point where the effort of taking that step becomes too much; it's just that not everyone is unlucky enough to reach it.

Hring and I had many of the same experiences. We'd both been oblates who'd grown up in a monastery; we'd both studied the Trivium and the Quadrivium in a monastic school. Sometimes we talked about the experiences we had in common — stumbling barefoot down the night stairs to chant the prayers for Lauds, struggling to learn Latin by listening to the colloquies, taking weekly baths in tepid water, learning to form letters and then words and then whole sentences on parchment in the scriptorium. Other men's thoughts to begin with, and then our own thoughts. My monastic life hadn't ended with ordination, but continued with scholarship until I was sent north to work in Elmet. His monastic life had ended in dishonor and expulsion for something he hadn't done and then he returned to his former home in Elmet like a disgraced castaway.

I'd known men like his novice master, men who used their authority to tyrannize boys who couldn't defend themselves, and sometimes worse. At least Hring had escaped that. When Hring had come home he had the experiences I will never have: marriage, fatherhood, life with his family on a *tún*. I looked at him across the table and saw how he'd changed in the last year. I remembered how he'd been changed when he came back from Eoforwic, wracked with guilt about leaving his children, still stunned by the loss of his wife. I could see now that his time working for the Mercians in the south had changed him again. He was harder now and capable of premeditated cruelty. That's how a man gets when he thinks that everything's been taken from him; that's how a man gets when he believes he has nothing left to lose.

Rumor isn't evidence. I sat at the table in Torhtmund's long house with the advocates and watched Ingulf watch Cwichelm, and I knew that Ingulf was convinced that his former assistant was bedding his young wife. I could feel his seething hatred and resentment, and so could everyone else at the table. He believed it. Absent evidence. Absent faith in his assistant. It was a rumor that had been started without malice a couple of winters ago, when Sentwine's *geréfas* were drinking together with some of the *geréfas* of Ingulf's *hird*, and they were mocking the old advocate's sense of self-importance.

Someone made a remark about Ingulf's new wife, a young widow called Thryth who had a small child. They all believed she'd married Ingulf only for the security of being wed to an advocate.

Someone made a remark about Cwichelm's courtesy to Ingulf's new wife, and else elaborated on it, then someone made a remark about Cwichelm, who they all believed was a pederast, and someone elaborated on that. They were drunk and amused by the idea of what a mismatch it would be. More beer was poured and more jokes followed, and as the night dragged on, the remarks were conflated and conjoined until what started out as drunken wit at midnight became a living rumor by sunrise.

Ingulf was quiet. He hardly took his eyes off his former assistant, but he was trying not to be obvious, so he was hiding his face behind the only thing available, the horn cup he was drinking from. Ingulf was drinking a lot, and excusing himself to have a piss and coming back to the table, and then drinking more. I was worried that he was working himself up to something unpleasant. Weddings are like that. Feelings that are buried most of the time work their way to the surface like festering splinters. All the drinking doesn't help. Anger is like anything else, the unpracticed don't know how to do it well, and Ingulf avoided expressions of anger, which meant that if he surrendered to the emotion the best we could hope for was that it would erupt in an embarrassing and inappropriate way, at the worst there might be blood.

When Mæl had invited the hird to his wedding he made a particular point of asking me to celebrate the mass and officiate the wedding. It was because I was with them in Northumbria, and it was an honor I couldn't decline. Since then, I'd been working on a sermon, and I told them that I had more work to do and excused myself from the gathering so I wouldn't be present if Ingulf created a scene. I trusted Creda and Sentwine to intervene if it came to that.

Outside, the *tún* and the home field beyond the wall were like a *gemót*. Men and women were walking around the grounds inside and outside the wall. There was a market street of tents and stalls set up against a length of the home field wall and the general mood was festive. I was amazed at how many guests there were. It looked like half the population of the hundred. What I knew of Hring's brother Mæl was that he was difficult to get along with. When we'd gone into Northumbria he'd been remote, wrapped in guilt because he thought he'd failed to protect Hring's son. He kept himself almost entirely in the company of Æthelwaru, who'd been with him when the killing *thegns* had come. I'd arrived at Hring's *tún* with the *hird* not long after they'd taken the boy, and it looked like a killing field after a battle. Mæl had nothing to be ashamed of, but he still believed he'd failed Hring.

That night in Northumbria, while we were waiting for dark to come, before we went into the *tún* where they had the boy, he and Æthelwaru had come to me and asked for confession. Hring was off watching the *tún* across the valley, and the rest of the *geréfas* were seeing to their kit and preparing for the coming blood work. No one knew how many of us would live through the night, but no one hesitated, and God was with us, and we all came through unmarked. I've thought about that night often in the last twelve months and wondered how unmarked we really are.

I looked up and saw Hring walking out of the long house and he saw me and turned in my direction. He moved carefully, like something feral that had to worry about surviving the day. I supposed that it had to do with spying in the south, and that it wasn't something that could fall away after only a few days back on his father's *tún*.

"It's good to see you again," I said when he walked up.

"I want to thank you for performing the marriage ceremony," he said. "My brother deserves some happiness in his life, and it means a great deal to him, or he wouldn't have asked you."

"Northumbria," I said.

He nodded and took a breath. We were both remembering that night in Northumbria. What I remembered was that I was the only one who hadn't gone mad. I wondered what he was remembering, possibly the shape and depth of his madness and the guilt that comes with enjoying it.

"It means something to me, too," he said after a moment.

"Do you want to confess?" I offered.

Hring smiled. "When I went to Eoforwic after Oswith died, and I was on the *frith stol*, they were always offering me confession, but then I had nothing to confess."

He looked away at the people who had come to celebrate his brother's wedding, ignoring my offer of the sacrament. I didn't push him.

"I'll be busy a while yet, so I won't have time to spend with the *hird* until after the wedding. I promised my brothers and sisters that I'd kill rats for them. My children are helping, so it's time I can spend with them."

I understood that time with his children was more important than time with us.

I said, "At celebrations like this you're stretched thin. No one will feel slighted."

He looked back at me and smiled and for a second he looked like the old Hring, and then the smile disappeared. "It's good to see you too."

Then he walked away.

Ꝺring

The afternoon before the wedding Derehild's half of the kindred rode out of the woods in a long train of horses and waggons in a billowing cloud of dusty, self-possessed entitlement, looking like they gotten turned around somehow on the road and had suddenly discovered a leprosarium were they'd been expecting a Roman spa and hot springs, and they were looking for someone to blame. It could have been that few revelers were there to make much of their arrival; there were dog fights and horse fights and cock fights on the other side of the *tún*, outside the wall. We could hear the clamor and the cheering through the trees. Even though she didn't want to be at the party, Derehild seemed insulted that the party had started without her.

My uncle Whitgar was riding at the head of the group. Whitgar was Derehild's second born and only son, but never let that get in the way of a good time, and he looked like he was primed to enjoy himself at Mæl's wedding no matter what his mother thought. Aside from Whitgar, Derehild had produced only daughters, and she'd molded them all in her own image.

I'd met their husbands at one time of another and they weren't bad sorts, just men who'd married unwisely into a nest of fractious bitches who'd adopted their mother's grudges as their own. At one time or another, at some drunken celebration, all of their husbands had admitted that after the wedding ceremony their sweet and biddable attitudes had rapidly curdled like left over milk in a sun-warmed bucket.

Derehild herself reminded me of some startling antiquity, a memento of a former time unearthed by accident in the course of a quotidian activity like digging a cess pit, that was now on travelling display like a curiosity from a lost world. She was enthroned in an ornately carved wooden chair packed with cushions that softened the jostling on her old bones, and shaded by an enclosing canopy. She looked as if she was present under unvoiced but well-understood protest, discharging an unpleasant duty that was necessary to avoid an even more unpleasant consequence if she refused.

I hadn't seen her in three winters, and I could have happily waited another three before I found myself once again in the presence of her reptilian stillness, looking into those glittering, unblinking eyes in their wrinkled sockets under white eyebrows. If a muscular forked tongue had oozed out of her mouth to taste the air I wouldn't have been surprised.

Her hair was covered by a brocaded wimple and her dress, dusty from the trip, was a deep green. She was wearing gloves that disappeared into her sleeves, leaving the impression that her hands and wrists were made of leather.

Derehild was accompanied by her daughters and grandchildren, all of whom looked like they resented having their routines uprooted. Only my uncle Whitgar called out a greeting and waved to those of us who had assembled to receive them. He spurred his horse out of position at the head of the train and cantered up to us and jumped out of the saddle.

"It's finally happening, eh?" he smiled and threw his arms around Mæl.

Very few people who hadn't grown up in the same house as Mæl would ever entertained the thought of embracing him, but Whitgar had known us all since we were boys and girls and felt an avuncular affection for us. "She's a fine woman," he said. "You're fortunate in your choice."

"Good to see you Whitgar," Mæl said as they struggled to keep their balance in the mutual embrace. "Bring the bearskin?"

"Of course," Whitgar laughed. "What would a feast be without the bearskin?"

The bearskin had belonged to a giant black

bear that had lived in the forest near Whitgar's *tún* when he was a younger man. When urged to hunt the bear down, he said that he had no quarrel with it, that it had lived there long before Whitgar came, and that he found bear meat greasy and the taste somewhat rank on the tongue. He concluded that so long as the bear left him alone, he'd leave the bear alone.

However, bears being uneducated in property rights, a couple of years later it had killed and eaten the home field boar that Whitgar'd been fattening and pampering to be the main course at the Yule feast. Content to lose a bit of grain and a tithing of windblown mast in his beech wood, and not begrudging the bear even the occasional beehive, the murder of his home field boar pushed Whitgar too far. He took a couple of spears and went into the woods to redefine their relationship.

No one saw the confrontation, but it must have been Homeric, because when Whitgar limped out of the forest a day later, he was wearing only one boot, his tunic was raggedly slashed into blood-stiffened tatters, his beard was crusted with dried blood, and a single iron spearhead was all that remained of both shattered spears, but he had the bearskin rolled up and thrown over one shoulder.

"Gave me a hell of a fight," was all he ever said about it. "I gave it a warrior's funeral — burned the carcass and left one of the spearheads for grave goods. A skinned bear looks a lot like a naked man."

He had the hide tanned and everyone thought it was going to become a wall decoration, or a rug, or a cover for Whitgar's high-backed chair in the hall, but when it came back from the tanner Whitgar dusted it with fleabane and set it aside in its own purpose-made cedar chest, where it remained except at the big feasts and celebrations when, after he was sufficiently drunk, he would put it on like a heavy winter coat and get down on his hands and knees to reenact the battle, entertaining the children, who would cluster around him and try to knock him over.

I think it was Whitgar's genuine enjoyment of the children's delighted reaction and his willingness to act foolishly that made him a favorite of each successive generation of the kindred. The rest of Derehild's line was too stiff-necked and encrusted in their belief that Old Torhtmund had somehow wronged them to unbend sufficiently to enjoy our company.

"How's Derehild?" Old Torhtmund asked.

"Derehild's Derehild," he shrugged. By which I understood that she'd spent the whole trip stewing in the bilious seepage of her usual foul mood.

The waggon stopped, and a thin cloud of dust swirled around us and then drifted away. Derehild looked straight ahead, held the rigid pose for a couple of seconds, and then deigned to look at us, as if she'd just noticed that she'd arrived.

"We're here, mother," Whitgar said. "Time to get down and start making everyone miserable."

"You're a constant disappointment," Derehild told him.

"Think of your reward in heaven," he said.

"No reward can make up for your inadequate devotion to me."

"Hello Derehild," Old Torhtmund said. "So good of you to come."

"Don't pretend that you didn't invite me just so I'd give your idiot son a gift."

Sprot leaned toward me and whispered, "She's a charmer."

"More charming every time I see her."

"Help your stepmother down," Flæd said.

Old Torhtmund stepped forward and extended his hand as Derehild used her walking stick to lever herself upright and took a step to the edge of the waggon bed. She batted his hand aside and nodded to Whitgar, who reached up and took her weight and set her on the ground. Derehild reminded me of a bird, substantial looking in her full plumage but hollow-boned and light enough to drift away on the wind if you plucked her; when she was standing on her feet beside the waggon the kind of bird she reminded me of was a buzzard, hesitating before it plunged its beak into a bloated gut. She spotted Mæl and took a couple of steps in his direction.

"Don't you hurt that girl," she told him.

"Why would I hurt her?" Mæl asked. "I'm marrying her."

"That's what men always say," Derehild snorted. "I've experience of marrying off daughters. They never choose wisely when it comes to a husband."

"Æthelwaru will be grateful for your advice," I assured her.

She turned her head without moving the rest of her body and looked at me. "*You*," she said in a tone that sounded as if it had been marinating in contempt for years.

I smiled at her. "Good to see you step-grandmother."

She'd never forgiven me for beating her grandson Lullo. He'd shown up to give Oswith the last rites and insulted her dead body. Not even after I'd paid compensation — which I'd thought was overpriced (it's not as if he'd known his Latin any better *before* I beat him) — but still, the Law's the Law. I scanned Derehild's entourage, but I couldn't see Lullo and I wondered what urgent pastoral duties had claimed his attention elsewhere. Then one of the mounted sons-in-law shifted in his saddle, and his horse took a step sideways, and I saw Lullo sitting a chestnut mare, about as far away from me as he could get; he'd been trying to keep out of my sight.

Derehild looked at Mæl again, and then at Old Torhtmund, and then she tottered away on Whitgar's arm.

Fastulf, the *tún-geréfa* who'd grown up on Whitgar's *tún*, showed them where to set up their camp. There were four waggons in the train: one for Derehild alone, whose august self-importance demanded privacy to marinate properly in her usual rancor, a supply waggon that contained their provisions and gear, and two waggons that were packed with Derehild's daughters and their children. The sons-in-law were mounted. I reckoned they spent enough time in proximity to Derehild's daughters to prefer saddle sores to the acrimonious chatter of their women.

By the end of the week, the home field had begun to resemble a siege encampment without the whores, the spontaneous guttings because of drunken dice games, or the camp flux. What had started out as a random assembly of tents pitched in the order of their arrival had matured into the sort of *ad hoc* community that emerges whenever people assemble for an event. I had the feeling that Mæl's wedding might appear in one of the local monastic chronicles as the milestone of the year, the kind of entry that often commemorates a particularly deadly cattle murrain or the death of some mystical hermit who talked to animals and after either a protracted, grisly martyrdom, or a long and virtuous life — depending on which biography you favored — was placed on the fast track to sainthood.

Musicians piped and harped and drummed; jugglers cascaded stones, knives, fruit, and axes; tumblers walked tight ropes, climbed slack Jacob's ladders, and did cartwheels, back flips, and handstands; a hasty market did untaxed business in the odds and sods that everyone had left home without; horses, chickens, and dogs fought to the death in their separate venues; food was cooked and consumed, liaisons were discretely accomplished in the green shadows of forest glades. There were even a couple of *mæsse-thegns* in attendance to absolve the excesses of the guests and urge a greater temperance, as is their wont, on the men and women who were allowing themselves a bit of relaxation to celebrate the wedding of the most irascible man in the hundred.

Whitgar

Things being what they are in my family, I don't see Torhtmund as much as I'd like. Our father died when I was five winters old and Torhtmund was seventeen. When Bryhtmund died, Torhtmund became more than a big brother to me, and we've never let the trouble between him and Derehild come between us. It hasn't always been easy, because there's always some punishment from mother for anyone consorting with a person from Ældgyth's line. It may come sooner or it may come later, but it always comes, often sideways, a punishment that targets someone you love with the clear message that their pain is your fault. Derehild's one to hold a grudge.

Derehild was Bryhtmund's second wife, and she came to help with the younger children of his first wife after she died. My memories of my father are fragmentary and vague, and he died before I could form a complete picture of who he was, so I've had to rely on what Derehild and my older step brothers and sisters have told me. Derehild's version has proven unreliable.

According to my mother, Bryhtmund's first wife was a harpy, and he was lucky to see her into the ground. According to Torhtmund, she had her faults like everyone, but she'd been a good mother. I think that what happened was that the traits and virtues that made Derehild an acceptable second wife made her an unacceptable stepmother. I love her after a fashion, and I suppose she loves me in her way, but I can see her more clearly now. Sometimes the way a mother loves her children and the expectations that go with that love are a greater burden for them to carry than no love at all. If I had a choice, I wouldn't be related to her. It sounds evil to say that about your own mother, but there it is. She's a vindictive and spiteful bitch, even if she did carry me in her belly for nine months. Derehild's never been a woman who could abide another's authority, and when Bryhtmund died, and his position as head of the household passed to his oldest son, Torhtmund, every day became a struggle.

I was too young to understand what was happening except that Derehild and Torhtmund were at odds. Then Godgyth died and everything unraveled.

Torhtmund and Werhard were gone from the *tún* performing their *brycgweorc* service. It was winter and the *ealdorman* had called them up to repair an ice-damaged bridge. At the beginning of the week they were gone, their youngest sister Godgyth, whose chore it was to milk the cow in the evening, slipped on ice when she was carrying the full bucket back from the barn and spilled the contents. It was an accident caused by the unbalancing weight of the heavy bucket and ice covered by a skiff of snow, but Derehild shut her up in the barn all night as punishment.

She huddled next to the cow in the straw for what warmth she could borrow, and that's where we found her the next morning, barely conscious, so cold she wasn't even shivering anymore. Her lips were blue and her skin was pale and waxy and tears had frozen to her cheeks like bits of broken glass. When she did talk, she mumbled slurred nonsense, her dress, soaked by the spilled milk, was frozen around her legs and when they brought her inside it cracked. She didn't recognize us or know where she was.

Sigmund and Sæwyn put her by the hearth fire, but instead of finding comfort in the warmth she began to writhe as if she were being burned, and then she started moaning. As her dress thawed we could smell the disgusting combination of souring milk and urine. She'd pissed herself sometime in the night, and it had melted the frozen milk and then they'd mingled and refrozen in the fabric. But even though she was inside the house close to the fire, she seemed to get colder, and then she started twitching and her arms and legs got rigid, and she shuddered, and then she died. My sister Godgyth was the first death I ever saw, and I'll never forget it.

When she died a silence deeper than the silence of winter light came over the house and we all sat still, listening to the fire burn down. Sigmund stood up and looked at Derehild and he started to breath heavily and his face got red and Sæwyn put her arms around him and held him and cried but he never took his eyes off Derehild, and we started to get scared that some violence was going to happen. It was a presence in the house, like death was a presence, both standing beside Godgyth's body.

Sigmund put on two tunics and his heavy cloak and went out to saddle his horse. Then he rode to find Torhtmund.

They didn't come back that night. Sæwyn and Cynehild stripped and washed their sister's body and dressed her in her best clothes and laid her on the table away from the hearth fire, with candles burning at her head and feet. Derehild collected her children about her and didn't offer to help. She must have known what was coming when Sigmund and Torhtmund returned. There was no meal that night and we all went to sleep hungry.

Sæwyn and Cynehild and Sigebehrt kept vigil with the body, the girls praying and crying, Sigeberht standing motionless, holding his sister's dead hand. It was an awful night. I tried to go to them, but Derehild kept me back. Edu was two winters older than me, and the rest of my sisters were all younger . . . they didn't even try.

Just after dawn the next morning, Torhtmund, Werhard, and Sigmund came through the door. Torhtmund and Werhard went straight to the table where Godgyth was lying and stood by her for a long time. Sigmund went back outside to see to the horses. I remember the shoulders of Werhard's cloak steaming in the warmth of the house. After a long while Torhtmund turned away from his sister's body and walked to the hearth. The fire was nothing but smoking, gray coals in the middle of the ash bed.

He broke up some kindling and used the small bellows to blow life into the coals. When he'd built up the fire, the only sound was the snap of the flames and the pop and crack of the cold wood burning. Derehild was motionless, watching him work with her children huddled around her. I struggled out of her grasp and ran to Torhtmund and put my arms around him and he lifted me up and held me.

"Godgyth died." I sobbed, and then it all came out, all the grief that I'd had inside but couldn't release when only Derehild was there to see it.

He rocked me in his arms for a little while and then he set me down beside the fire and said, "Derehild."

My mother then made the mistake that changed the course of all our lives. "It was her fault," she said. "The clumsy girl shouldn't have spilled the bucket of milk."

"This household is dissolved," Torhtmund said.

"You can't dissolve the household," Derehild shouted. "I have a right to stay here with my children."

"Stay," Torhtmund said. "And much good may it do you."

"Then what do you mean, dissolving the household?"

"My brothers and sisters and I will leave here as soon as I've built a new *tún*. You can keep this place. It's poisoned for us now. One-third of Bryhtmund's hidage is yours by right of law. I'll put it to the *ceorls* to stay or go with us as they please. Your guardianship is restored to your kindred. I'll keep the guardianship of your children until they reach legal age, but they're still Bryhtmund's children and under the kindred's *borh* for the rest of their lives."

At the time I was unaware of the substance of what Torhtmund told Derehild. It was only later that the details took on shape and importance. Then I just knew that nothing was ever going to be the same, and that the changes that had begun when our father Bryhtmund died were now complete.

Torhtmund called the *ceorls* together that afternoon. There were nine families living and working on the *tún*. Seven of them chose to go with Torhtmund.

Over the next five weeks, as the winter deepened and the weather turned colder still, Torhtmund and his brothers and the *ceorls* who took their household salt from the family cleared and began to construct the new *tún*. By the time the weather turned and the ice broke up on the river Calder they'd relocated, leaving Derehild to manage as best she could on the *tún* that was now ruined by Godgyth's death.

Osgiva

I could hear father calling me but I was with mother and I didn't answer him. I was laying on the grass beside the standing stone with my ear to the ground like I used to lay with her in the bed sometimes listening to her heart, but there was no heartbeat in the ground. Sometimes when I dreamed her we talked, and sometimes we played in the grass in the meadow above the home field. I liked to hold the white dandelion balls up where the wind could pull them apart and watch the seeds scatter in a drifting cloud and sometimes she would blow on them when there was no wind and they'd swirl around my head like snow and get in my hair and on my eyelashes. Mæthild and Torhtmund and Gulhere all said that she came to them in dreams, but she came to me the most; she came every night, and I told her what happened during the day, and she told me what to do to be a good girl.

Last night I told her that I was starting not to remember what she looked like when I was awake, even though I knew her face when I dreamed her; she said that was all right, that she would always look like she looked when I closed my eyes, and she would always remember me because I was her little girl. She said that even if the home field was full of people, that even if everyone who lived in Loidis and Eoforwic and even Londinium were in the home field, and even if it was a moonless, foggy night, she'd be able to find me, and I'd be able to find her in the middle of all of them, so there was nothing to worry about if her face got faint when the sun was up and I thought about her.

But even though she told me that last night, I wanted to see her in the daytime, too, so I got up early, when only the sun and the cows and the *ceorl* who does the first milking were getting up, and I came out to the standing stone and laid down with her the way I used to do sometimes when father was gone at the *gemót,* and I would lay beside her and listen to her heart.

When she died and father went away, we went to live at Old Torhtmund's *tún* where father had lived when a little, before he went to Eoforwic, and when he came back, before he met mother. Old Torhtmund is father's father, and Flæd is father's mother, and Mæl is his brother. The other uncles and aunts are his brothers and sisters, but Mæl is his special brother. Mæl said.

Mæl said that when they were little boys Hring kept him from getting bitten by an adder that was stretched out in the sun on the warm rocks in the stone wall around old Torhtmund's home field. Father saw the adder and hit it with a stick, and it crawled into the wall. Mæl said that he was four years older, but he didn't see the snake, and the snake would have bit him, and he probably would have died.

Mæl said that ever after that he was afraid of snakes because they can be anywhere, and you don't see them until it's too late, so forever after that father was his special brother. And Mæl thought it was his fault when father went to the minster in Eoforwic — that they gave his little brother to the church because Mæl had been bad — and he prayed and promised that he'd be good if they'd just bring father back, but they didn't bring him back. And once, when Old Torhtmund went to Eoforwic, Mæl went with him but the monks wouldn't let them see Hring. Mæl had brought father a smooth, speckled river stone so father would remember him, but the monks said father couldn't own anything, even a smooth speckled river stone, and Mæl had to bring it home again. He told me he'd was afraid father would forget him.

I knew how Mæl felt, because I was afraid mother would forget me, and that's why I told her what Mæl had told me about the adder and the smooth stone when I dreamed her last night. She said that all happened a long time ago, and father didn't even remember the snake. But I knew he remembered the smooth stone.

Mæl collected smooth stones wherever he went, but they were all in his mill covered with dust, and Hring was the only one he ever wanted to give a stone to.

When father was away after mother died, Mæl came to see us almost every day after he was done working in the mill. He would come and play with us at old Torhtmund's *tún,* and his mother Flæd, who's our grandmother, said once he didn't have to come every day, and if he wanted to help he should go to Eoforwic and bring father back, but Mæl said that father would come back when he was ready to come back, and he wouldn't thank any of them if they went after him. Until father came back, Mæl was going to come and see us as often as he wanted and tell us stories about father so we wouldn't forget him.

But we all wanted to forget father because he left us when mother died. We all hated him, and when we thought of him it was like a stone where our hearts are, making it hard to breath. And even though we wanted to forget him, we all thought of him and wondered what he was doing, and if he'd forgotten us, because we thought maybe he wanted to forget us because we reminded him of mother.

But Mæl said father was a drunk in Eoforwic, and he was trying to forget everything because he loved mother so much. Mæl said he'd never had anyone that he loved that much, and he said he thought father must hurt more than it was possible to live with hurting. Mæl said that it was only when you love someone as much as they'd loved each other that you could live when the person you loved died, and that if father needed to be drunk for a good long time to forget all his pain and remember how much he loved us, then that's what he had to do. He said pain's the measure of love.

Mæthild and Young Torhtmund didn't believe him, but I did. Gulhere was too little to understand. I thought maybe the pain we all felt because he'd left us was the measure of how much we loved him.

And Mæl came almost every day, and sometimes he took us fishing in the pond on his mill, and we would make a fire and cook the fish and eat them, but only the fish Mæl didn't know. Some of the fish he'd been catching and letting go for so long that they were his friends, and he wouldn't let us eat them. And sometimes we would stay in the mill when it was raining, and Mæl would show us all of his smooth river stones and tell us who each of the stones reminded him of, and why, and where he'd found them, and what that day had been like.

Flæd said that she felt sorry for Mæl, because all he had was river stones instead of friends, but I knew that all of the stones reminded him of real people, and that we each had stones there in the mill for Mæl to remember us so he wouldn't be lonely when he was grinding flour.

And then Mæl met Æthelwaru one time when he took us to the market in Loidis. She was with her brothers, and they were buying chickens, and Mæl told them which chickens they should buy if they wanted eggs and which they should leave alone unless they just wanted to eat them, and her brothers told him to shut up because he didn't know anything about anything except grinding corn. Mæl said he was going to teach them a lesson about what he knew and what he didn't know, but Æthelwaru got between them and said her brothers didn't know which end of a chicken the shite came out of and that everything he said was right, and asked him how did he know so much about chickens?

Mæl told her when he was little his job was to take care of Old Torhtmund's chickens. Æthelwaru's brothers said why didn't Mæl and his children go away and leave them alone, and Mæl said that we were his brother Hring's children, who assisted the advocate Sentwine, and he was watching us for the day.

Æthelwaru asked him didn't he have children of his own? Mæl said he didn't have a wife, so he couldn't have children. And one of her brothers asked him if he knew what a bastard was, and Æthelwaru said if he didn't all he had to do was have a look at her brothers, and Mæl and Æthelwaru laughed, and when I told mother about it that night she laughed too.

Mæl still came to see us, but one day when he usually came he didn't, and the Dog Man told me that he was going to see a woman lived Calder-side, and we guessed that it was Æthelwaru. Then Mæthild told Mæl that maybe we could all go somewhere and see Æthelwaru because we liked her too, and that's how we all helped Mæl and Æthelwaru get handfast.

We would go to the woods to look for mush-rooms, or to our *tún* to visit mother, or to Loidis on market day, and Æthelwaru would meet us and they would talk and later on sometimes they'd kiss. Once, when we were at the mill, Mæl showed us the stone he had for Æthelwaru. He kept it apart by itself on a beam, where he could look up at it and not have to try and find it in a crowd of other smooth stones. It wasn't the big-gest or the smoothest or the one with the most pleasing shape, but Mæl said it was the favoritest of all his stones.

When I told mother all about Mæl and Æthel-waru, she said she was glad for Mæl because he was big and rough and he scared people, and eve-ryone thought he was stupid, but he loved us, and he made sure he was with us now that she was dead and father was a drunk in Eoforwic, and he deserved to have love in his life. She said Mæl had always been her friend, and she thought he was funny and sad and she never worried about father or us when we were with him because she knew Mæl would never let anything bad happen to us.

That time those men came to kill father, and tried to kill us instead, and took Torhtmund north, Mæl and Æthelwaru killed most of them. Ordgar helped. And then father and Mæl and Æthelwaru and father's friends went after the ones who took Torhtmund ,and they killed them and brought Torhtmund back, and still Æthelwaru's family didn't want Mæl to marry her. When I asked mother about it, she said they were afraid of Mæl because they didn't know him as well as we did, but that Mæl and Æthelwaru would get married in the end because they were already married in their hearts.

I spread my arms and pressed down on the grass by the standing stone and hugged mother, and told her I loved her and that I missed her and I wished she was here for Mæl's wedding. She told me that when she was alive she met Æthelwaru once, but they hadn't been friends. She said if her children thought Æthelwaru would be a good wife for Mæl, then she knew Mæl would be happy.

Then I could hear father coming closer, and I said goodbye to mother and told her that it was time for me to get ready to go to Mæl's wedding. I stood up and father saw me and came into the cemetery where mother was sleeping alone, except for our little brother Hring, who was born dead and never talked to any of us because he'd never learned to speak.

"I was worried when I couldn't find you," father said.

He walked up to mother's grave and put his hand on the standing stone, the way he always did when he went there, like he used to touch her shoulder when she was alive.

"I was telling mother about Mæl's wedding, and that we'll miss her there," I said.

Father nodded and took my hand.

"Did you talk to her last night?"

"I told her I was afraid I was going to forget what she looked like."

"You'll always be able to see her when you close your eyes and think about her," he said.

"That's what she told me too," I said.

"It must be true then," he said, and picked me up and carried me back to the house.

"We have to get something to eat now," he said. "Because after, we're going to put on our best clothes and go to Old Torhtmund's *tún* for the wedding."

Ðring

Mæl's **wedding day** dawned clear and mild. The air was still and the sky was cloudless and larks sang in the meadow. All the omens were propitious, if you believe in that sort of thing. I was just happy it wasn't raining. The dry and festive encampment would quickly turn into a sucking swamp of bad humor after a few hours of rain, and I wanted Mæl and Æthelwaru to have better memories of their wedding than the smell of wet wool and sneezing guests and muddy hems and boots.

The children and Eadgiþ and I stayed on our *tún* the night before. Mæl stayed with us so he could use the bath house, and I had the tub filled with fresh water and the bath house fire built high to heat it. He spent a couple of submerged hours in the bath, scrubbing off the month and a half since his previous immersion with a boar-bristle brush and perfumed soap purchased in Loidis especially for the occasion. We could hear him splashing and singing, a noise like a bear with its hind foot caught in a deadfall deciding whether to keep trying to pull himself free or just chew his foot off so it could escape. When he was finished he came out of the bathhouse wrapped in a great length of cloth and a fleece and shook the water out of his hair and stood looking up at the moon in the early night sky.

I had my bath then, while the water was still warm and soapy, and then Eadgiþ and the children had their baths, and by that time the water was cooling, and we let the fire die. After we were all clean and wearing clean clothes, we ate, and after Eadgiþ put the children to bed, Mæl and I walked around the *tún*.

"The fockers," Mæl said.

"Who?"

"Everyone who talked bad about you when you went to Eoforwic after Oswith died," Mæl said. "The fockers."

"I shouldn't have gone," I said.

"You did what you had to do," Mæl stopped and leaned against the top of the stone wall with his forearms taking his weight and looked out over the dark home field, thinking, and then he straightened up quickly and stepped back from the wall, brushing something invisible from his sleeves.

"It's only now I understand why you did it."

"Then explain it to me," I said. "I don't remember deciding to do it. I just remember noticing I was doing it and not caring. I left my children."

"I watched them for you," he said. "We knew you'd be back."

"I'll never be able to repay you for that," I said.

"Naught to repay, brother."

"Then tell me why I did it."

"Because you couldn't live the life you were living without her. Children, work, the *tún*, she was the center of everything."

"You're right. But I still shouldn't have left the children."

"Regrets are good. But you did what you needed to do; good or bad don't signify. It's done, and feeling bad you had to do it won't change it."

"Then I had to leave them again."

"We all understand about that, too" he said. "The *focking* Mercians. What you're doing now you're doing for Elmet and the kindred."

There was a pause while we stood there, looking out into the long twilight of the early summer night listening to the chirping of the crickets.

"I hope you're as happy as we were," I said.

"That only means I'll suffer as much as you did when it's over."

The next morning we got up and washed the sleep away and dressed in our best clothes. Osgiva was missing from the house, and after a search round the *tún* I found her sitting on her mother's grave. She was worried that she was forgetting what her mother looked like, but I told her that she'd always remember Oswith and I carried her back to the house to get ready.

We walked across the home field together. Eadgiþ and me and Mæl and the children. It took longer than usual because Mæl was spinning the children in circles at arm's length as he walked, each of them taking turns and laughing as they got dizzy and then wobbling after us through the meadow grass waiting for their next turn. He let Young Torhtmund carry his *lang-seax*, the blade he would present to Æthelwaru to keel safe for their sons to use when the time came, and my son walked with the scabbard over his shoulder, feeling his importance as blade bearer.

When the guests saw us coming they came out to greet us and accompany the groom to Old Torhtmund's house. It was midmorning, and there was no sign yet of Æthelwaru and her family.

Unlike the hapless groom in the stories, a nervous wreck celebrated in embarrassing and ribald detail, Mæl was as calm as a moonlit pond. His brothers were exhibiting all the usual anxiety, worried that something might happen at the last moment to undermine the day. Gosfrith had posted runners far down the road to alert us of the bridal party's approach, but midday came and went without a sighting, and my brothers grew more apprehensive until we saw a runner pounding up the road, feet throwing up puffs of road dust, waving his arm as he ran.

"They must be coming," I said to Gosfrith. "You can relax now."

He said, "I'll relax after they've jumped the broom."

I climbed onto the top of the wall and watched the wedding party approach Old Torhtmund's *tún*. Wulfnoth was leading them, riding erect on a powerful looking horse, an embroidered cloak around his shoulders and a silver pin sparkling erratically on his shoulder as it caught the light. His sons were riding behind him, and behind them a line of waggons jostled up the rutted road. The bed of the lead waggon was enclosed by a frame hung with linen curtains that swayed with the movement of the waggon's lurching progress. Ribbons hung from the top of the frame; garlands of flowers and ivy were wound around the four corner posts. The linen curtains were embroidered with figures I couldn't make out at that distance. The waggon was drawn by a matched team of white horses, and one of Æthelwaru's brothers was driving it. A second waggon contained Æthelwaru's mother and sisters, and a third waggon held their children. Æthelwaru's father rode ahead of the first waggon, and her brothers flanked it.

They approached at a stately pace.

Mæl drew himself to his full height. He was a head taller than the next tallest man in the party, head and shoulders taller than most of the rest, and he looked more like a monumental statue in fancy dress advertising a tailor shop than my brother. I searched my memories of him for a time when he had seemed happier, but I came up with nothing. He was wearing a completely new outfit: tunic, pants, cloak, belt, and boots—the lot—and both arms sparkled with polished silver rings. I'd never seen him wear so much as a finger ring. His hair, freshly washed and barbered, was long over his shoulders and stirred a little in the breeze.

As the bridal party drew closer and the drapes fluttered erratically apart with the motion of the waggon I could see Æthelwaru sitting on a large, throne-like chair in the waggon bed. Some of the children ran beside the waggon throwing handfuls of flower petals into the air; the colored petals caught the breeze and drifted in a cloud to settle on the horses and the driver's shoulders and cling to the linen. Mæthild had told me about the petals; they'd been her idea, and I could see that she was proud of the effect, running beside the waggon with a basket in the crook of her left arm, laughing and smiling as she tossed bits of color into the air.

The waggon passed through the gates of the *tún* and turned toward the family chapel, where the priest waited at the door. The crowd of guests lined the way, cheering and calling out to one another and drinking in the kind of celebratory revelry that I knew could get out of hand at any second.

Wulfnoth stopped his horse at the chapel door and dismounted, and Old Torhtmund embraced his childhood friend, and they exchanged some quiet words.

Eadnoth, Æthelwaru's father, was swaying in the saddle as he reined up in front of the church door. Three of his sons quickly dismounted and hurried to help him climb down from his horse. Eadnoth must have weighed twenty-five stone, and it took a moment for them to steady the horse and support him as he swung his right leg over the back of his saddle and the horse's croup, and then he lowered himself onto the box they'd placed under the stirrup.

Eadnoth stretched and turned around to face us, nodded at Old Torhtmund and Flæd, looked at Mæl for a long moment (did he sigh or did I imagine that?) and then walked back to the second waggon to collect the women of the family. Two of his sons repositioned the box beside the draped waggon bed and then stood by the horses. The driver set the brake.

The little girls hurried to position themselves around the box, upon which Æthelwaru would step in her descent to the ground. The waggon shifted as Æthelwaru stood up and steadied herself, and then she pushed the linen drapes aside and stepped to the edge of the waggon bed. Flower petals rose into the air and fluttered around her face and she stepped down onto the box and her brothers helped her to the ground.

Æthelwaru was dressed in a white linen gown and her hair was bound with a wreath of flowers and ferns. The hem of her gown was decorated with tablet weaving and embroidery, and as she stepped down from the waggon bed I could see that her soft leather shoes were decorated with blue beads. She looked around the crowd and smiled and waved in a flurry of petals. I understood at least part of the reason why Eadnoth had been disagreeable during the marriage negotiations: Æthelwaru looked at least twelve months pregnant. Her belly strained against the linen, and she cradled it in her hands as she stepped off the box.

"Uh . . ." I began as I turned to my sister Elfilda.

"It looks like Derehild got that one right," my sister whispered.

The priest Jaruman was waiting for Mæl and Æthelwaru at the door of the chapel. Eadnoth escorted his daughter to her place on the left side of the door (because woman was made from a rib on Adam's left side) and she never took her eyes off Mæl, who stood on the right side, facing Jaruman in the chapel door.

They exchanged gifts, symbolic sods and the *lang-seax*, transacting the business of the marriage first to get it out of the way. When that was accomplished Jaruman moved on to the ritual.

"Does anyone object to this wedding?" Jaruman asked, managing not to look at Æthelwaru's immense belly as he spoke.

There was a long moment of silence, during which my brothers glowered at the crowd, afraid that there might actually be someone out there who had the balls to raise an objection at this point. If anyone had, I wouldn't have given them good odds on surviving the afternoon, but after Jaruman had extended the opportunity to object long enough that Gosfrith was twitching with anxiety, he asked the same question of the bride and groom.

"Do either of you know of any reason why this ceremony should not proceed?"

There was a pause, and then Mæl and Æthelwaru said "No," simultaneously, as if they hadn't realized they were being asked. Apparently no hints of consanguinity had emerged during their lengthy engagement, and the obvious evidence of sexual compatibility was being assumed without comment for the record.

Jaruman smiled and said, "Mæl will you have this woman to be your wedded wife, will you love her, and honor her, keep her and guard her, in health and in sickness, as a husband should a wife, and forsake all others on account of her, and keep only unto her, so long as you both shall live?"

"I will," Mæl said, a bit louder than I expected, as though he wanted the people in the back of the crowd to hear.

Jaruman turned to Æthelwaru. "Æthelwaru will you have this man to your husband, will you love him, and honor him, keep him and guard him, in health and in sickness, as a wife should a husband, and forsake all others on account of him, and keep only unto him, so long as you both shall live?"

"I will."

Jaruman nodded to Mæl, who turned and looked at Æthelwaru.

"I Mæl, take you Æthelwaru, to my wedded wife, to have and to hold from this day forward, for better, for worse, for richer, for poorer, in sickness, and in health, until death do us part, if the holy church will ordain it. And thereto I plight thee my troth."

Æthelwaru said, "I Æthelwaru, take you Mæl, to my wedded husband, to have and to hold from this day forward, for better, for worse, for richer, for poorer, in sickness, and in health, till death do us part, if the holy Church will ordain it. And thereto I plight thee my troth."

I heard my brother Gosfrith sigh, beginning to relax for the first time in a couple of weeks.

"Rings?" Jaruman asked.

I took the two rings out of my bag and handed them to Jaruman, who handed the larger one to Mæl and the slightly smaller one to Æthelwaru.

Æthelwaru extended her left hand and Mæl slipped the ring on her first finger and said, "In the name of the Father", then on her second finger and said, "In the name of the Son," and then on her third finger and said, "And in the name of the Holy Spirit." Then she did the same.

Jaruman extended his hands and touched the tops of their bowed heads.

"I bless this marriage in the name of the Father and of the Son and of the Holy Spirit, and let these two dwell as one from this time forward, amen."

Mæl and Æthelwaru looked up.

"You're married," Jaruman announced, and a cheer erupted from the crowd as Æthelwaru put her arms around her husband and kissed him, a little awkwardly, over the unborn child in her swollen belly.

Then the families went into the chapel for the wedding mass.

We are all of us many people simultaneously, without giving it conscious thought. In many cases, people we know in one context wouldn't recognize us if they heard us described by someone who knows us in a different context. The color and texture of our likes and dislikes and attitudes about life change subtly depending on whom we express them to. The act of watching changes both the watcher and the watched.

I thought of that as I watched Mæl and Æthelwaru avow their love and desire to wed their lives together. To most of the people who know him, Mæl is a gruff, opinionated giant who grinds your corn and criticizes your life choices, but to Æthelwaru he's Furry Badger. To her family, Æthelwaru is a razor-tongued bitch spinster daughter with a violent temper and poor impulse control, but to Mæl she's Little Bunny.

To some I'm a former novice in the minster in Eoforwic, to others I'm an assistant advocate in Sentwine's *hird*, to some a spy in Brorda's clandestine service, to others still I'm just a ratcatcher. I'm a father to my children; a brother to my brothers and sisters; a son to my parents. Only Oswith had seen all of me, known the integrated and disintegrated fragments of all the men I was and am, and hadn't seemed confused or put off—possibly she knew me better than I knew myself from the advantage of her objectivity, whereas I, like everyone who comes to self-knowledge from a place of subjective disadvantage, know only the least distasteful version of who I am.

Æthelwaru and Mæl seemed to know one another in a way that no one else had taken the trouble to discover, and that mutual knowledge had joined them together, as the halves of a thing combine to create a wholeness. I'd had that myself and lost it, and I felt its absence. I wished them years together, and more happiness in every one of them than they had in the last.

When **Mæl and Æthelwaru** came out of the chapel into the sunlight, with the rest of the wedding party following close behind them, the crowd of guests, assembled expectantly around the chapel door, well-primed by the beer and mead they'd been consuming throughout the wedding mass, began to cheer and dance in their excitement, perhaps allowing themselves to be carried away by a collective fantasy in which Mæl was transformed by the love of the woman he had chosen and who had chosen him, and by the grace of that mutual love would no longer berate others about the condition their lives or harangue them about the inevitably disastrous results of the choices they made or didn't make, or their affinities or inclinations or disinclinations, or chosen vocations or amusements, or their selection of clothes, or techniques for worming their sheep or plowing their fields or tending their orchards or harvesting their grain, or wiping from back to front instead of front to back; perhaps even that Mæl might adopt a calm and generous mode of discourse in keeping with his newly sweetened nature.

If so, it was a lesson in how a virulent delusion can sweep through a crowd when it allows its vigilance to lapse in a celebratory moment under the influence of the hot sun and strong drink, because an hour of marriage had not diluted his capacity for the withering observation, offered in a true spirit of innocent, neighborly generosity.

The young daughters of the kindred crowded around Æthelwaru and once more the air was filled with a colorful blizzard of flower petals. I wondered if there were any flowers left unplucked within a mile of the *tún* and how far afield the bees would have to range to find sustenance. What would be the impact on their honey production, and on the subsequent fermentation of mead?

Æthelwaru walked with a slow, rolling pace, her left hand cradling her swollen belly and her right hand on Mæl's arm. The crowd parted ahead of them, and they made their way down the slope toward the gate of the *tún* and the beribboned pavilion beyond it in the center of the home field. Well-wishers lined the path and offered toasts, those in the front ranks to the couple's happiness, those deeper in the crowd to certain bawdy events that lay ahead of them (as well as certain bawdy events that had already come to pass), together with speculations about the nature of the morning gift. It showed good sense, however much beer had been drunk, to make these speculations from out of reach in the depth of the crowd, because although Mæl had a sense of humor there was no telling what his response to a joke at his expense might be at any given time, certainly not on his wedding day.

The wedding procession left the *tún* and started across the home field, which had been thoroughly mucked that morning to save the bride and groom from the embarrassment of treading on the random excreta of the home field boar. The grasses were growing in the absence of the sheep and cattle that generally kept them grazed short, and the stalks whipped my ankles as I walked behind Mæl and Æthelwaru, poised to catch her if she lost her balance on the uneven ground. I think we were all relieved to step under the thatched pavilion roof onto the level footing of the boards and walk the length of the trestle tables to climb the two steps to the dais and take our places at the long head table.

For a wedding feast of such a size (by my hasty reckoning there must have been between two and three hundred guests), everyone in the family had contributed the services of their cooks and table servants, and Creda had convinced the *ealdorman* to loan us his cup *thegn* to try to impose some order on the organization and preparation of the food. Ordinarily I wouldn't have given much for his chances of harnessing seven cooks who were used to running their own kitchens, but the ceremonial importance and sense of occasion that hung over Mæl's wedding drew them together, and they submitted to the cup *thegn's* supervision, so that the expanded cooking facilities had been bustling with activity for two full days before the feast.

The Dog Man had to kennel his pack because the smells were urging them toward a feeding frenzy that even he couldn't suppress. Older children were detailed to guard the finished cakes and tarts from the depredations of their younger brothers and sisters as well as from drunken guests drawn by the tantalizing smells.

The feast was a complicated series of courses that was served and removed in a sequence meant to enhance the taste and experience, punctuated by palate-cleansing drinks, but as the courses continued to come, one after another, they finally began to blur together like the dog's breakfast: swans and geese; grilled, poached, and baked eel and fish; roast pig, lamb, and venison; mutton and mushroom hotpots; meat pies, fish pies, vegetable pies, casseroles of dove and lark breasts and wild grains; oysters, prawns, and crabs; platters of beef and pork ribs swimming in tangy sauces; breads and cakes; tarts; platters of minced tongue and sausage; pork, mutton, and beef pies baked with chunks of dried pear and apple; cheeses and eggs; fruit puddings—and to drink: wine for the diners at the head table and ale, beer, mead, small beer, and cider for the guests.

The head table was decorated with wreaths and greenery and candles. There were green glass decanters for the wine supported by stands made from heavy silver. Clear glass cups from the Rhineland were emptied with every toast. The large wheel of cheese I'd been given by the cheese master at Wokenduna priory for killing the dairy rats was on display in front of Æthelwaru's father. I wondered how much would be left when

Eadnoth was finished with it. But the most amazing feature of the head table decorations was placed in the center, between Mæl and Æthelwaru—a representation of Mæl's *tún* and mill, the buildings made of toasted slices of bread, the mill pond and race filled with white wine. Creda's cup *thegn* had outdone any wedding confection I'd ever seen, and it was the focus of much admiration.

As the food was being served, the priest Jaruman rose to give the first toast. It was a variation on the same theme that he'd expounded on in his homily at the wedding mass: 1 Corinthians 13.

"'If I speak in the tongues of men or angels, but have not love, I am a ringing gong or a clanging cymbal.'" Jaruman looked over the wedding guests in the pavilion and shrugged. "It's clear that Paul never met Mæl." There was a pause while the audience tried to cope with such a declaration. Then Mæl boomed out a laugh and a second later the guests joined him.

"But Mæl is not without love. If anyone's love can move mountains, it must be his. Paul said that love is patient and kind and doesn't boast and isn't proud. Would anyone who knows Mæl describe him that way? And yet he is full of love. And would Æthelwaru's family say that she is not easily angered and that she keeps no record of wrongs? Yet she is full of love."

"No arguing with that," my sister whispered, her eyes on Æthelwaru's pregnant belly.

"Faith is belief without proof, but this wedding

is the proof of their love, and the faith they have in one another, and we can all believe the evidence of their love. Often marriages are made without love. There are many reasons for marriage, not all of them good or honorable. Sometimes love grows within such a marriage, but more often it does not. Those marriages are pale reflections of marriage, but they are undertaken for lesser reasons. This marriage is a true marriage, where husband and wife know each other and are fully known. *Wassail.*"

Everyone cheered and emptied their cups.

After that, man after man, the head of every household present rose at his place and reached into his word hoard for wishes for happiness and long life and healthy children for the married couple and after each toast cups were drained and everyone cheered. Throughout the toasting and eating, guests delivered presents to the head table and Mæl and Æthelwaru thanked them and they were set aside. Mostly the gifts were monetary (shillings in small bags), or on the hoof (a goat, a lamb, a pig, even a rooster), or some portable household good (a mortar and pestle, shears, scissors, a mirror, a set of loom weights), or personal, like the cloaks that my girls had woven for Mæl and Æthelwaru (which they received with such abundant thanks you'd have thought they were woven silk hemmed with gold thread). Then Rud approached the table carrying a large covered box that he placed on the floor in front of them and whipped off the cloth like a magician revealing his signature trick: Rud's special surprise gift.

A monkey the size of a dog was sitting on its haunches in a wicker cage, a tail as long as the rest of its body wrapped around itself. It reacted to its sudden revelation and the accompanying gasp from the wedding guests with a nervous bark, hopping to its feet and pacing in the cramped box, its hands gripping the wooden bars like a prisoner in one of the *geréfa's* lock holes. Its fingers were covered with hair but instead of claws like every other animal it had fingernails on its unnervingly human hands. Rud opened the hinged top of the cage and the monkey climbed out and up his arm onto his shoulder, wrapping his tail around Rud's neck and slipped its fingers into his hair, looking around at all the babbling faces.

I'd only ever seen drawings of monkeys, but they hadn't prepared me for the reality of a monkey. Most of the wedding guests hadn't even seen drawings, and a spontaneous intake of horrified breath spread through the crowd, together with a few stifled squeaks from the fainter hearted. People made the sign of the cross and their lips twitched in muttered prayer.

On its feet, the monkey was a couple of feet tall and weighed maybe two stone. He had a black face, but the fur on his back, arms, and legs was dun-colored, blending into whitish gray fur on his belly. The monkey's black-tipped tail was as thick as a snake. When he shifted position on Rud's shoulders he displayed ball sack covered in bright blue flesh between his legs, and his dick was as thick as my thumb and redder than sunrise.

After a moment he calmed down and began to search through Rud's hair with long, dexterous fingers until he found something interesting there and picked it out, examined it, and popped it into his mouth, chewing briefly. The monkey had two pair of long, sharp, curved fangs, top and bottom, and when he yawned it looked like he wanted to eat your soul.

"I didn't know you had a son," Mæl said. "I see the resemblance."

It was one of the few times I ever saw Rud at a loss for a sharp retort, or if he had one, it was obscured by the nervous laughter of the guests, who were deeply unsettled by the monkey. They might have heard that monkeys existed; they might have heard a monkey described, but confronted with the reality of a monkey, like some monstrous fetal nightmare that ought to have been exposed on a rocky, sleet-blown heath instead of allowed to live, they were all profoundly disquieted, torn between the revulsion that their religious training urged and the curiosity that their human nature demanded.

"Thanks for the gift," Mæl said. "When we look at it we'll always be reminded of you."

We all felt a faint sense of relief when Rud put the monkey back in the cage and carried it away. I watched the people he passed struggle with conflicting urges to have a closer look and the impulse to draw back. Rud set the monkey on a table on the side of the pavilion and opened the top of the cage, and then he tied one end of a long leather leash onto his collar and the other end around the post, and then Rud went back to his seat.

A little while later I noticed that the monkey had climbed up the post and was sitting on the rafter. A small group of boys had taken up positions under him and were looking intently into the shadows above their heads. I suppose paying close attention to a monkey was a lot more interesting than watching the wedding guests give Æthelwaru and Mæl gifts and listening to drunken toasts about wedded happiness and the desirability of marriage.

It was during the prolonged gifting phase of the feast that I noticed the *tún-geréfa* Frod, drifting along the edge of the pavilion with a cup in his hand and his eyes fixed on some point in the crowd. I followed his line of sight and spotted Eadgiþ talking to some of her friends from before she went to the convent. They were mostly married now, a few of them probably had their own children, and she was engrossed in the conversation, which was punctuated by frequent laughter.

Frod found a spot where he could lean against a post and watch Eadgiþ almost without blinking. I could see that there was a subtle and disturbing kind of menace about it, like a snake watching a mouse. I wondered what he was thinking, and then I realized I didn't want to know. I looked at Eadgiþ, who seemed unaware of his scrutiny, and when I looked back again at Frod he'd disappeared into the crowd.

The feast dragged on. When the presents had all been given, and the last platter of swan's liver pâte scraped clean, the inner rows of tables were taken down to make room for the dancing, and the musicians took up their places and began to play. Lines of dancers began to weave around and between the blazing fires in the three stone hearths to the rhythm of the harps and the hand drums and the flutes.

After everyone had exhausted the topic of Mæl's marriage to Æthelwaru, and her profound pregnancy, which took a couple of hours, conversation devolved into the topics that everyone was most comfortable with.

Gosfrith was holding forth about swine. He was an acknowledged expert on pig husbandry, widely recognized as a man who knew how to use everything on a pig but the oink, and he was often pestered for advice by lesser swine lords whose hogs had the squirts, or whose weaners wanted to get back on the teat, or whose pannage was unsatisfactory. When talking about swine Gosfrith was a man transported, like a philosopher explicating an epistemology that had evolved over a lifetime to his eager disciples.

Oswith's father was advising men on their bee hives. My brother Tilmund was talking about the virtues of iron as opposed to leather door hinges. My brother-in-law Scenwulf was talking oxen. No one was asking me anything. My absence was mysterious and people knew enough about the reason for it to know not to ask more, which left me free to ghost through the feast more or less unmolested by boring conversationalists.

The young unmarried girls were taking advantage of the opportunity to dance with the young unmarried boys under the supervision of mothers and aunts and married sisters, and they were swirling in a circle as the flutes played and the drums pounded the rhythm. As I watched them, thinking that maybe Sprot's sister Somerild might like to dance, I saw Eadgiþ in conversation with Frod on the opposite side of the pavilion.

Whatever they were saying, Frod appeared not to like what he was hearing. His posture was tense and his distance from Eadgiþ was closer than she seemed to like because she kept backing away and he kept moving closer to maintain a dominant proximity. Their voices must have been only loud enough for them to hear each other because the people closest to them, clapping and watching the dancers, were paying no attention.

Then Eadgiþ said something definitive, shaking her head, and she made to turn away, but Frod reached out and grabbed her arm to stop her. She threw off his hand and I stood abruptly, ready to go over there and advise him that if he put another hand on my youngest sister he'd be wearing that hand around his neck on a cord.

Frod leaned close and said something and Eadgiþ slapped him. I started toward them and then stopped when I saw Sprot materialize out of the darkness behind them and put a hand on Frod's shoulder.

Frod seemed taken by surprise and said something sharpish to Sprot, who smiled and leaned closer and said something in return. Frod's head jerked back and he said something even more sharpish that must have had more than a hint of threat about it, because Sprot reacted like a Eoforwic street *geréfa* and spun him head-first into a post, held him steady for a moment, leaned in and said something else, and then slammed his head twice more into the wood. It happened so fast amidst the noise of the dancing and the singing and the drums that no one noticed but Eadgiþ and Frod. Sprot stepped to the edge of the pavilion floor with Frod and they faced into the darkness standing side by side, Sprot supporting the *túngeréfa's* dazed weight, and then my friend treated Frod to a final demonstration of his Eoforwic street interview technique and tripped him off the platform, face first into the darkness.

Again, no one seemed to notice, or if they did, they weren't disposed to interfere. Scuffles at weddings are as common as runny noses in *Hréðmónaþ*.

Sprot stood there for a moment looking down at the ground outside, and then he turned and said something to Eadgiþ and held out his hand and she took it and they merged into the circle of dancers and spun away.

Sprot had always had a soft place in his heart for women in distress, and a great sensitivity to their needs. He must have observed the unfolding drama between Frod and Eadgiþ and read the story of the tension between them. He was more or less handfast with a woman in Eoforwic, a woman called Juthwara he'd grown up with in the down-river village of Acaster, who'd been working as a whore called Rowan when I'd met her—although, according to his sister Somerild, Juthwara had been promoted and now occupied a management position that required no time on her back. I reckoned it might not be long until I was going to Eoforwic for *his* wedding.

That immediate threat to the *mund* of Mæl's wedding feast averted, I sat down and started talking to Oswith's parents, Teowulf and Osthryth. It was good to see them again, but I sensed a faint, lingering disapproval of me going to Eoforwic and drinking for eight months. I didn't blame them, I disapproved of it myself, but before I could make it right I'd been dragged off to work for Offa.

"We often visit the children," Osthryth told me.

"Mæthild looks more and more like Oswith," Teowulf said. "Have you noticed?"

"Every time I look at her."

Osthryth gave her husband one of those wifely looks, as if she were worried that his observation might set me on the road to another half year's drunkenness. I'd been the occasional object of those kinds of looks from her daughter, and I recognized it at once. We were all still grieving Oswith in our own ways, and what I'd learned about grief, drunk and pissing myself in Eoforwic, was this: grief can't be denied; grief can't be ignored; grief can't be overcome; grief can't be hurried; grief can only be endured until you and grief are done with each other.

I was about to tell them to be easy, that although I'd grieve for Oswith the rest of my life, I thought that grief was nearly done with me, and I wasn't about to relapse into drunkenness (at least not the sort of chronic drunkenness they were worried about, although at Mæl's wedding acute drunkenness was a definite possibility) when there was a commotion in the direction of the cluster of tables that Derehild's side of the family had occupied.

They took up nearly a quarter of the pavilion, with Derehild in the center, enthroned in the chair she'd arrived in, which the sons-in-law had unfastened from the waggon bed and placed at the table to mark the center of their territory in the pavilion. For all I knew she hadn't left the chair since her arrival—maybe there was a hole in the seat so she could piss.

I'd been keeping my distance from them because I knew that Lullo was there somewhere and I didn't want to provide even a flimsy justification for some unpleasantness at the feast. Mæl might be safely married and out of their reach as gossip mongers (although I reckon there was a lot of self-congratulatory "I-told-you-so" whispering about Æthelwaru's pregnant belly), but I had undeniably beaten the rat-fock out of Lullo and provided Derehild with an unforgivable insult to brood over until she breathed her last malevolent breath. I wasn't going to give her an opportunity to make an issue of it here.

However, the voices were getting louder, and they had the recognizable cadence and tone of a disagreement, so they had my attention as soon as I heard them.

"It's time to give my toast," I heard a man say, barely louder than the surrounding babble. From the condition of his delivery I was sure he'd been toasting long and deep all afternoon and evening; there was a struggle, and up popped Lullo, shrugging off his mother Edu's restraining hand.

All talking in the pavilion didn't stop, but silence collected over the tables where Derehild's side of the kindred was sitting, which caused the guests on the periphery to turn their attention to the drunken *mæsse-thegn*.

"This can't be good," I said, and Teowulf and Osthryth looked at one another and prepared themselves. They knew what Lullo had said when he came to anoint their daughter's cooling corpse.

Lullo was an embarrassment to the kindred, but he was an especial embarrassment to anyone who was descended from Derehild, making the sting of his indiscretions that much more painful for them to endure. He'd been shipped off to a monastery soon after Old Torhtmund had delivered me into oblation in Eoforwic because Derehild wasn't about to be outdone in piety, but Lullo didn't take to monastic life as well as I had. When I was expelled, it became a point of pride that he be ordained, giving Derehild a success where I'd given Old Torhtmund a failure—at least that's how she'd seen it. Lullo was just another pawn in the chess game Derehild was playing with Old Torhtmund in her head. The tragic joke was that Old Torhtmund wasn't sitting at the board, so she was playing that game with herself.

When Lullo returned as a priest who could barely stumble through the Latin of the mass and the prayers in his psalter, his spirit was broken. While I'd recovered from my disgrace, Lullo never recovered from his success, and he took to drinking to elevate his mood. I'd tried that when Oswith died, and it hadn't worked out any better for me.

Derehild insisted that he perform the duties of *mæsse-thegn* for her side of the kindred, but he did them so poorly and erratically that they looked elsewhere for whatever spiritual guidance they required. The only reason Lullo had come to anoint Oswith was that my *tún geréfa,* who'd been sent to fetch the *mæsse-thegn* who usually attended us, had found him gone and, understanding the urgency of the moment, had collected Lullo instead, reckoning that *in extremis* a priest was a priest was a priest.

Lullo stood quietly, probably waiting for the pavilion to stop swaying, and then he squinted in the direction of the head table.

"First Epistle to the Corinthians," he said. "'It is good for a man not to have relations with a woman.'" Lullo stopped abruptly, swayed a little and put his hand on the table top. "I reckon that advice is a little late."

"More bible quotations with commentary," I sighed. "How fortunate we are to have Lullo explicate St. Paul for us." For a moment I'd hoped that Lullo was going to attempt something spiritually uplifting. There are some good things in First Corinthians that make it a favorite wedding scripture (Love is patient, Love is kind), and Jaruman had already mined it for inspiration, but Lullo skipped the thirteenth chapter and jumped ahead to the seventeenth, where Paul had set forth his ideas about celibacy and carnality.

"To avoid fornication, every man should marry."

That didn't come out the way St. Paul had meant it, or maybe it had, Paul being a blatant misogynist. I could see traces of a rueful recognition among Derehild's sons-in-law, who were no strangers to withheld sex.

"The wife hath not power of her own body, but the husband. Likewise also the husband hath not power of his own body, but the wife." Lullo forged ahead, but then he seemed to lose his place and skipped a verse, continuing, "I would that all men were even as I myself—"

"What, shitefaced?" A voice from the back of the pavilion called out, and there was a scattering of involuntary laughter. This was the sort of social misjudgment that people come to a wedding hoping to see, and everyone in the pavilion was beginning to pay attention to Lullo's extemporaneous sentiments.

Lullo wasn't used to having a heckler in his audience. Most of the time his congregation was happy to let him follow his homiletic babbling to as rapid a conclusion as possible so they could get on with their lives. He hesitated and turned to peer in the direction he thought the voice had come from, but whatever thread he'd intended to follow was rapidly unraveling.

"Every man hath his proper gift of God," he said after a moment, but it didn't sound like he was convinced.

"We know what yours is," the voice called out.

Lullo's father stood up and stared into the back of the pavilion, a discouraging scowl on his lips, but if he thought he could intimidate drunken hecklers into silence when they had as easy a target as Lullo, he was mistaken. Then the thread of his discourse snapped and Lullo left the well-trod exegetical path of the wedding homily and, bewildered and adrift, struck out on his own through the wilderness of First Corinthians.

"Is any man called being circumcised?" he thundered. "Let him not become uncircumcised. Is any called in uncircumcision? Let him not be circumcised."

"Thank God for that," someone else called out.

"Circumcision is nothing—"

"It is if you've got a dick," a third voice interrupted to general laughter.

"And uncircumcision is nothing, but the keeping of the commandments of God."

Sprot was sitting across the table, beside Teowulf, and he turned to me and said, "I thought we were going to have a toast."

I looked at the head table where Mæl was focusing all his attention on his step-cousin, and his wife had laid a cautionary hand on his arm.

"Now, concerning virgins," Lullo said, raising his cup and taking a sip.

"Wait for it," a voice called as Lullo recharged.

"I have no commandment of the Lord: yet I give my judgment. It is good for them if they abide even as I. But if they cannot contain, let them marry: for it is better to marry than to burn."

There was some random applause as Whitgar made his way through the tables and drew up in front of Lullo. Whitgar's expression was dark, and his face was red as he struggled to keep his voice down yet still convey the magnitude of his displeasure in a way that would penetrate Lullo's shitefaced urge to speak. Lullo said something that Whitgar evidently interpreted as sass and he put his hand on Lullo's shoulder so that his thumb lay on the big nerve near his collarbone and squeezed suddenly and as hard as he could. Lullo's eyes rolled up into his head and his knees buckled and he sank back onto the bench. There was a final bit of urgent conversation, and then Whitgar stood up straight and waved to everyone and thanked them for their attention. A few people booed and a crust of bread arched through the air and bounced off Whitgar's back as he returned to his seat.

"That came off better than we had any right to expect," I said.

"What was that about?" Sprot wondered.

"Who knows," I shrugged. "At least it was all from First Corinthians."

Saul of Tarsus was a hard core evangelist, as if he felt that he had to compensate for a Roman father and a collaborating Hebrew mother, or maybe for not having been open to the good news when Jesus was still alive and therefore excluded from the gang of twelve, or possibly because he'd hunted Christians for the Pharisees. His epistles reek with an eloquent petulance that he was never reluctant to employ when he was browbeating a wavering congregation. His terse remarks about marriage are a good example. He thought that single men and women, widows and widowers, ought to remain celibate, like him, but if they couldn't resist their baser animal urges, then they should marry, because marriage is better than roasting in hell for eternity because you got it off with someone you're not married to. For Paul of Tarsus, at the moment he wrote that thought down at least, marriage was just slightly better than a never-ending ass roasting in a supernatural inferno.

I reckoned that Lullo had been sitting there, getting drunker and drunker, working on some convoluted insult that he intended to cloak in the respectability of a few New Testament quotations, and a mashup of Paul's first letter to the Corinthians — that favorite of the nuptial sermon — had risen to the surface of his befumed brain like a gassy corpse after a few days in a slow moving river.

I looked at Mæl and Æthelwaru. The danger of Mæl squeezing Lullo's head off his shoulders with one hand had passed, and now they seemed as amused as everyone else by Lullo's extemporaneous sermonizing. It was a good thing Lullo hadn't managed more coherence; it was beginning to look like we might just escape the feast without some great disaster.

Then the advocate Ingulf walked up to me and said, "Have you seen my wife?"

The Monkey

The monkey was far-travelled. He'd been born on an east African savanna, where he'd been taken as an infant by a Kikuyu hunting party after they killed his parents for camp meat, and, because he was too little to make a decent meal and cute on top of it, traded north to a Somali, who traded him farther north to an Persian from Hormuz, who'd traded him further north still to a Jew from Akka, who'd given him to his niece, whose husband promptly lost him in a dice game to a Greek sailor the night before the Greek shipped out to Aleppo to pick up a shipment of Lebanese cedar. Because the monkey could climb the rigging with greater dexterity than any of the sailors, the crew made him their mascot and gave him the run of the ship. The sail maker tailored a smart little outfit for the monkey: a little pair of trousers (crotchless, so he wasn't trapped in them with his excrement and to display his bright blue ball sack to advantage) and a jaunty hat with a debonair gull's feather.

From Aleppo the ship sailed to Heraklion, where the monkey changed hands in another dice game and three days later took another ship east, this time to Antioch. The monkey's new owner was a morose, discontented man who enjoyed sporadic luck at dice but who spent his off-duty hours drinking and complaining to the monkey, who he found to be a more sympathetic listener than his human shipmates. The monkey was still free to climb the rigging, but the crew lost interest in that trick after a couple of days, despite the careless flare the monkey projected due to his flashy attire.

After a quick turnaround in Antioch, the ship cast off for Syracuse with a hold full of pepper. The third night out the monkey's new owner offered him a drink. The monkey, only just feet tall and weighing only a little more than two stone, was much disadvantaged in his ability to match the man cup for cup and rapidly became gibbering, shite-flinging drunk, and—made vertiginous by the slightest movement of the ship under his feet—beguiled the crew with his unsteady shambling across the deck, tail lashing spastically about in a quest for balance. After that the monkey and his owner became steady drinking companions, and their nightly binges were a reliable evening's entertainment: much coin changed hands in wagers on who would fall over first. Before they made port, the monkey had become addicted to the ecstasy of daily liquid communion with his simian god, and had rediscovered his drunken sea legs.

Luck abandoned the sailor in Syracuse, and the monkey acquired a new owner, after which he was traded three more times, becoming increasingly famous for his drunken antics as he worked his way north up the Italian peninsula from owner to owner in city after city, abandoning his roughly tailored sailor's clothing along the way for the more elegant Italian couture of red silk, open crotch trousers, a jeweled leather collar, a sumptuous purple velvet hat, and a matching embroidered vest.

He was sold to a luxury goods merchant and collector of curiosities in Napolis and sent to live in the family villa on Capri, but while he was there he escaped when, in a bad mood brought on by his new owner's hard-hearted insistence that he give up drinking, he bit his owner's sadistic young son—who delighted in pulling his tail up so he could flick at his blue nut sack, pendant through the open crotch of the silk trousers—and disappeared over the wall of the villa. After three days on the loose, foraging in the scrub of the highlands with only marginal success—which ruined his outfit and put him in a foul mood—the monkey made his way down to the harbor village and charmed his way onto a boat that was returning to the mainland. Possibly it was the tattered silk trousers and leather collar studded with polished lapis that sealed the deal.

He stayed in a townhouse that belonged to the master of a pottery guild for a few months in Naples before being given to a Roman moneylender in partial payment of a debt. In Rome, the monkey became a secondary attraction at a well-known brothel called the House of Peacocks that was patronized by the decadent lesser sons of the nobility, merchants specializing in second-quality goods from disreputable Moroccan bazaars, and rank and file clergymen on pilgrimage — deacons, priests, and brothers; bishops frequented a more palatial brothel on the Esquiline. The wine was good, and he was allowed to drain any abandoned cups in the hall. One of the whores incorporated him into a number of sex acts performed for the prurient amusement of the customers that the monkey didn't completely understand, but all of which ended happily.

Then one drunken, calamitous night the monkey dozed off on a shelf and experienced a series of troubling dreams, the most troubling of which involved clinging to his mother's back as she scrambled toward the black trunk of an acacia tree, under which she'd been gathering seed pods, just ahead of a hungry Kikuyu with a spear. In a spasm of terror, the monkey's tail accidentally swept a large cruet of lamp oil off the shelf and onto one of the peacocks below. The bird was startled by the shattered cruet and splash of oil and hopped aside, sweeping its oil-soaked tail into a candle flame. The takeaway lesson for the monkey was that nothing spreads fire through a packed brothel on a Saturday night more quickly or efficiently than a terrified peacock with a flaming tail, screeching and careening like a panicked phoenix through a succession of gauzy door hangings meant to discourage flies.

The monkey woke to discover the brothel engulfed in flames and a frenzied riot of naked whores and their customers scattering into the night. Driven by its African instincts to climb to safety, the monkey hurried to the roof where it was trapped by the conflagration of the lower floors and forced to leap from the burning building to a clothes rope stretched between the brothel and the adjoining tenement and swing to safety.

Two days later, a wealthy Frank on a spiritual pilgrimage meant to ease his feelings of moral crisis and debilitating guilt caused by the source of his wealth (dealing in young slave boys to be sent to an appointment with castration in Verdun) discovered the singed simian begging for food near the Coliseum and treated it to a meal and a bottle of wine. The Frank was mesmerized by the monkey's blue ball sack, which he interpreted as a sign to remind him of the source of his guilt. When the monkey woke up he found he was hung over and chained in the back of a waggon heading to Ostia and a ship for Gaul.

The monkey passed his transit through Gaul

unsuccessfully trying to solve the enigma of the locked brass chain that held him captive. He crossed into Francia, where he expanded his palate of beverage preferences to include a taste for beer and ale. The Frank sold him to a Frisian trader from Dorestad who wrote to Gisl to see if there might be a market for an exotic pet in the Northumbrian court, but when he arrived in Eoforwic, Rud decided that the monkey would make a perfect wedding gift for Mæl and bought him from his father.

Rud liked a good, twisted joke, and he was amused by the image of the giant Mæl with the small monkey riding on his shoulders while he worked at the mill. Which is how the monkey avoided being gawked at by Northumbrian *thegns* in Eoforwic and was instead being gawked at by drunk wedding guests and brutish children in Elmet.

Wulfnoth

Wulfnoth **knew that feasts** aren't just about eating; eating is often the least of it. Feasts are about rank and status, wealth and pride. How many courses? How much meat? Is there sufficient variety, and what's the quality of drink? How is the relative importance of the guests revealed by who sits approximate to the head table, and who sits approximate to them? A feast can be a celebration, but it can also be the covert engagement of competing forces, with winners and losers, and although blood isn't often spilt, there is always the possibility that it might be. The dynamics of the feast are the dynamics of festivity and happiness, but they are also the dynamics of power.

Wulfnoth sat there smiling and eating and drinking what was served to him, but he was unstuck in festivity, drifting from feast to feast in his life, eating the venison that was served at his

wedding and drinking the beer that was served at
the birth of his first son; savoring the beef that was
roasted at the wedding of his daughter, the
mouthwatering lamb that was cooked in rosemary
for the baptism of his first grandchild — unmoored
in the slippage of winter into winter, feast into
feast, like whispers in church or sighs in the dark
before sleep, directionless.

He looked around the pavilion at feasting
guests, possessed by celebration, sitting back on
the benches to let out their belts, sitting forward
with their elbows on the linen runners that covered the boards, sleeves rolled fastidiously back or
with gravy-stains, tablet-woven hems, fists around
horn cups, bobbing Adam's apples as they swal-
lowed, hair tied back or falling forward to frame
their faces as they bent their heads to empty a
spoon or to ply their knives, cutting, stabbing,
bringing a bite to their lips impaled on an iron
point that yesterday had cleaned the mud from
the sole of a boot or gutted a hare or severed a
rope or cut the umbilicus of a new son or daughter.

When it was clear that Æthelwaru was pregnant, her father Eadnoth had wanted to break the
betrothal and appeal Mæl for rape, but Wulfnoth
refused. "Get over it," he told his son. "Your
mother was carrying you in her belly when we
were married, and what was good enough for us
is good enough for our granddaughter." He
thought the fat shite stain was going to have a sei-

zure when he told him that, all black-faced with frustrated anger, but there was nothing he could do if he ever wanted to be the patriarch of the kindred.

A sea of brown hair, red hair, blond hair, white hair, black hair, islands of baldness like weathered stones exposed by a slack tide, dappled with sweat, shining in the firelight as the evening progressed, spread before him. After the formal toasting was done and the dancing began, then the informal toasting began. Drunken inspiration made tongues as golden as the mead and beer that washed over them (or so their owners thought) — touched by the genius of the moment, becoming orators and high priests in the private temples of their ecstatic, sodden minds — and they delivered inspired but enigmatic sermons in praise of love.

Wulfnoth sat at the head table, watching it all, the jostling for tactical position, and the strategic arrangement of groups within groups within represented kindreds. He was insulated by his age and his patriarchy, and the crumbling shield wall of his attachments to life and relationships to his blood kin around him.

There were gaps in that shield wall as memories and identities and relationships fell away, and the knowledge of himself and everyone who was not himself became doubtful and he felt his tight grip on who he begin to slip. He felt himself becoming insubstantial and transparent, the reality of who he was replaced by an idea of who he might have been, which, like all ideas, was different for everyone, and finally unknowable as the original became indistinct and unavailable for reference.

And that ghastly monkey the Frisian had brought with him from Northumbria, like a demonic and hideous spirit, something that looked like the condensation of the soul that lurked at the core of every cruel and mean and unpredictable man Wulfnoth had ever known, was the invisible essence of ugliness made real. Well, that was a Frisian's sense of humor, wasn't it? — the ability to see that as a joke and the willingness to inflict it on an unsuspecting crowd.

And then that *masse-thegn*, drunk and spewing bile into the room like convulsive vomit, had left the stink of his words lingering over their heads like a rancid mist. That *masse thegn* was from the side of the kindred that hated Æthelwaru's husband and his family, the one who Torhtmund's son the advocate had beaten shiteless. The desiccated matriarch who sat like an toad on a warm rock was the radiant source of that hatred; Wulfnoth could feel it rolling off her.

Æthelwaru leaned close and kissed him on the cheek. "Thank you grandfather."

She'd visited him every morning until she was too pregnant to ride, and still once or twice a week when she could persuade or bully one of her brothers into bringing her in a cart. She cooked for him, and washed his linen and clothes, and talked to him about whatever frayed strand of thought caught his attention, like a tatter of raw wool quivering on a gorse bush in the breeze. He told her long, disjointed truths from his life and stories about sons and daughters and brothers and sisters and his mother and father and his wife. Sometimes about the importance of lost opportunities that were shouldered aside by tangible facts. Wishes and hopes and dreams sometimes had equal weight and were indistinguishable from one another — things done or said by a son or a brother ascribed to a daughter or a sister, the hard-earned wisdom of a parent attributed to the innocent utterance of a child.

Æthelwaru was the last shield in the wall that stood between him and the irresistible solitude of his decline and fall.

More and more frequently he found himself thinking not in fragmented sentences or even discrete words that informed a thing, but in impressions and feelings, the residue of inexplicable and immediate experience, in emotive reaction instead of premeditated action, in colors and palpable sensation in his heart or his gut. He thought about a blind woman he had known as a child, her light stolen by the backward kick of a cow, sealed inside herself, able only to listen to life going on about her, unable to examine its colors and motion, and he thought he understood her imprisonment, and then her imprisonment and his understanding both melted away, and her blindness, and then the memory of the woman herself, leaving Wulfnoth sitting at the head table looking out over the heads of the dancing people in the pavilion that sheltered his granddaughter's wedding feast, feeling the impact of their dancing feet through the floor under his stationary feet, recalling him momentarily to the present.

He was full for the moment. The goose had been particularly good, everything he'd hoped for, and the chestnut and mushroom stuffing had just a hint of rosemary and crunchy onion that his wife had never added before, but that gave it a more textured flavor he approved of. He'd have to remember to tell his wife how good it was.

He stood up.

"Grandfather?"

"How would it look if I didn't dance at your wedding?"

Beside him, Eadnoth closed his eyes and shook his head, both dreading some spectacular embarrassment and hoping for an unambiguous example of his father's incapacity to head the kindred, something admissible at the *witangemót*, some behavior so demonstrably insane that his petition for the acknowledged patriarchy of the kindred could not be denied.

"I can't dance," Æthelwaru said, rubbing her belly with both hands.

"I know," Wulfnoth said. "But that doesn't mean I can't." He walked behind the benches at the head table and stopped behind Old Torhtmund's wife, Flæd, and put a hand softly on her shoulder. The wife of his boyhood hero turned and smiled at him.

"My wife isn't here, and my granddaughter can't dance," he said, certain only of those facts and not the reasons for them. "And so there's no one for me to dance with."

Old Torhtmund clapped him on the back. "See you have her back by midnight," he laughed and winked at Wulfnoth, and for a moment they were fourteen again, counting the days until they got their iron, making jokes about girls.

Flæd stood and offered him her hand.

"Wulfnoth was always the best dancer among us," Old Torhtmund told her. "Always the first on the dance floor at the harvest festival and the last one to leave it. All the girls wanted their turn."

"He got into trouble for it once," Wulfnoth said, talking fast to keep up with the memory unspooling in his mind's eye, narrating the story as if he were watching it happen to someone else, sensing that if it outpaced him and he lost the thread of it, he'd be standing there with it unfinished, the ending unknowable, his mouth empty of words. "He was dancing with a girl who had a fight with a man who was courting her and she wanted to make him jealous. The man was drinking and he came after him with a short *seax* and he had to fend him off with a stool until the man's friends could drag him away to cool off and get sober."

"What happened?"

"He finished the dance and married the girl."

"I'm sorry she's not here to dance with him to-night."

"So is he," Wulfnoth said. "But he thinks she wouldn't mind if he danced with you instead."

Flæd and Wulfnoth stepped out onto the boards and stood for a moment, letting the rhythm of the dance and the music wick up their legs until their feet were tapping with it, and then they joined the whirling dancers as they circled the blazing hearths, spinning over the boards, skipping and dipping, swimming in the music of the celebration of the joining of kindreds.

Wuldric

Everyone **had forgotten** about the monkey in the excitement of the feast except the crowd of boys who'd been drinking small beer and cider all evening and couldn't take their eyes off him, enjoying that combination of revulsion and fascination produced by something truly beyond the experience of their ordinary reality. They gathered below the monkey, who'd made himself comfortable on a rafter high above the revelers, and they were watching his every move, and when his roving glance met their eyes they felt the delicious chill of contact with something truly alien. All their lives priests had told them stories of the demons and imps that tortured the souls of the damned, and secret adherents to the old religion had told them stories of elves and forest spirits that lay in wait for the unwary in the deep *weald*, and the monkey seemed like some horrific combination of those two terrible manifestations of malignancy, congealed un-expectedly in their midst. The boys were particu-larly riveted by the monkey's genitals: a blue ball sack and a bright red cock in vivid contrast to the light gray fur that covered the rest of his loins.

On the monkey's end of things, there was only thirst and boredom and the gaggle of jabbering boys that had collected below him like flotsam in the sea of annoying noise. The monkey was a long time over being perplexed by the chattering of humans, their constant jabber of incomprehensible noise, and he'd learned to ignore the sounds that more than four or five humans produced when they gathered together. So long as he had plenty to drink, the monkey was happy to let them jabber at each other to their hearts' content.

The monkey, who'd been renamed by each new owner and who regarded each new name as merely another noise made by the human who provided him with beer or wine or ale, lounged on the rafter and watched the wedding feast with disdainful skepticism and an eye for the main chance. The people were eating and drinking and talking in a babble of noise, but they were rarely parted from their cups, and the servants were at-tentive to the pitchers of beer or ale or cider from which they refilled those cups, but the monkey was thirsty, having eaten his fill of wilted vegeta-bles and dried apples (not to his taste, but filling), and he watched the wedding guests closely in case one of them abandoned a cup of beer.

The man who'd brought him on the last leg of the trip, red haired and red faced and usually a reliable drinking companion, whose scalp could nearly always be relied on to yield up tasty little bugs for a snack, was seated far away across the grass-roofed pavilion. The monkey shifted his position and scratched his balls. The boys sitting below him laughed.

Wuldric watched the monkey closely and noticed that the monkey's eyes followed the movement of anyone who was drinking.

"The monkey's thirsty," he told Tilwald.

Tilwald looked at the monkey and saw a bored monkey absent-mindedly scratching its balls. "How can you tell?"

"It's watching anyone who's drinking," he said. "Pay attention."

Tilwald, with no eye for subtle clues of anthropoid behavior, watched the monkey and saw a monkey. "Let's give it some water," he suggested.

"Fock water. Let's give it some mead," Wuldric said.

Tilwald recognized an unspoken order when he heard one and wandered off to find an unattended cup. He was back in less than a minute. Wuldric stood up on the bench and extended the cup toward the monkey, tapping its rim on the rafter to get the monkey's attention.

The monkey looked down at Wuldric and stopped scratching his balls. Often the vicious little shite that he'd bitten on Capri had offered him a cup of liquid and then snatched it away, a game the boy liked to play that made the monkey angry and spiteful, and — sure enough — when he was about to close his fingers over the rim Wuldric moved the cup out of reach and laughed. Wuldric extended the cup again and once more withdrew it beyond the monkey's reach, and then a third time. The monkey sat still and looked deep and hard into Wuldric's eyes, and Wuldric, made uncomfortable by the humanlike familiarity of the stare, in which he recognized a pitying and disapproving intelligence, offered it again and allowed the monkey to take it.

Whatever was in the cup smelled warm and sweet, but the cup was cool to the touch. The monkey sniffed the contents and then put his face into the opening and kissed the honey-colored surface and tasted mead for the first time. He decided that although the noises these men made were different from the noises of other men he'd known — incomprehensible human gibberish all — they made a drink that he'd been waiting all his life to discover.

The monkey lapped the sweet mead until the cup was empty and then drained the last few drops into his open mouth and tossed it down to the boy. Honeyed warmth spread through his whole body nose to tail. He made the noise he made when he wanted more, a noise that sounded like a dog barking on the other side of the *tún*. Wuldric and the boys all copied the noise, barking monkey talk to each other, and the monkey knew they were mocking him, but even so they seemed to understand what he wanted because one of them went to refill the cup. Another one made a long series of pathetic mouth noises at the monkey until the boy returned with a full cup that the monkey nursed in long slow sips, letting the warm vapors of honey wine fill his head. He relaxed against the post and enjoyed the comfort of the two or three dreamlike images of Africa that remained in his memory that had nothing to do with his mother running for the acacia tree, while below him the shaggy heads of dancing men and women undulated like the surface of a rough sea, their long hair flying away like spindrift in a gathering gale.

The monkey pulled himself upright on the rafter and waited until the room settled and the warm flush left his head and then brought the leather leash to his black face and bit through it with a single, severing spasm. Then he rose on his hind legs and walked = across the rafter, his thick tail extended for balance.

The boys underneath laughed and clapped and monkey-talked to him, imitating his deliberate walk and sounding to the monkey like a troop of idiot monkeys with head injuries attempting sarcasm.

The monkey was a veteran climber who'd perfected his skills on the rigging, spars, and masts of heaving ships where, even drunk, he'd managed not to plummet to his death on the wet deck, so a stable rafter beam was the same as a wide Roman pavement to him, even as the mead circulated with vertiginous speed through his system, warming his belly and fingers and toes and clouding his vision with a transient, shining blur. He gripped the edges of the beam with his opposable toes and, his long tail swaying behind him for balance, waddled across the span without spilling a drop as the boys followed along eight feet below.

The monkey climbed into the shadows near the roof peak where the green smell of fresh thatch was strong and where nice snackable bugs were crawling around. He wedged himself into the intersection of the rafters and had another sip of mead. When he felt the growing pressure of a liquid fist clenching above his loins, he squinted down at the cluster of boys and located the one who'd offered and snatched away the cup. The monkey stood up on the beam and relaxed his full bladder, pissing into the air, something that had always made the sailors laugh but scattered the boys underneath in a cloud of shouted gibberish as the yellow stream plunged from the darkness onto the upturned face of the boy who'd taunted him.

"That focking monkey's pissing on us," Wuldric shouted as he twisted aside, sputtering the rank taste of monkey piss out of his mouth. He threw his cup into the rafters, but it was deflected by a beam and fell among the dancers' feet be kicked, clattering, across the floor and away into the darkness outside the pavilion.

A nearby table of guests had seen the monkey piss on the boys and they were helplessly sobbing loud, mead-fueled laughs to the boys' discomfort. The guests were at that stage of celebration where anything they thought was funny incapacitated them, stealing their breath and their ability to speak, until the ruthless mirth abandoned them to watering eyes and aching sides.

Wuldric gave them a murderous look and led his group of followers away. Outside the pavilion, Wuldric and his entourage walked toward the *tún*. "That focking monkey's dead," he promised, wiping his face and hair with the tails of his tunic. The shock of a stream of hot monkey piss hitting his face had burned away the effect of all the beer and cider he'd drunk and he was angry and more sober than he'd been since the late afternoon.

His younger cousins followed at his heels, all of them splashed with piss, but some of them not minding the discomfort so much because they secretly enjoyed the fact that Wuldric had been the one directly pissed on, and they were smart enough gloat about their secret satisfaction. Wuldric led them through the open gate toward the family tent so he could shove his head into a bucket of water and change into a tunic that didn't smell of monkey piss. Their route took them near the Dog Man's kennels.

Ordgar

O rdgar and his cousin Engelhard had been
watching Wuldric and Tilwald from a
wary distance since the conclusion of the
wedding ceremony, alert to the danger of
some reprisal in their personal feud. Since Engelhard had punched Wuldric in the face a year ago
in Loidis (after which Hring head-butted Engelhard to balance the equation) four more unwit-
nessed altercations had occurred and Engelhard
was currently one up, so they were expecting
some sort of retaliation before the night ended.

Engelhard had wanted to draw young
punk Wuldric outside alone, where none of his
group of hangers-on could see, and then beat him
preemptively senseless, but Ordgar knew that
Wuldric wouldn't part from his fawning younger
cousins, who were providing that attention all bul-
lies crave, and even if he did, most of the senior
Lawmen of Elmet were attending the wedding

and would rightly interpret any premeditated violence as a *mund-bryc* of Old Torhtmund's *frith* and deal with it accordingly. Ordgar kept his distance from Wuldric and made sure that Engelhard did too, but Ordgar was also wondering how he might entice Wuldric to break the peace in a publically undeniable way that would land him in the shite. When the monkey pissed on Wuldric's face, Ordgar had a cup to his lips and laughed so hard that cider shot through his nose.

"Let's follow them," Ordgar said when Wuldric and the other boys left the pavilion.

They slipped into the darkness with the pavilion between them and Wuldric and walked quickly around the exterior, hidden by the circling mass of dancing guests. They were slowed momentarily when Engelhard tripped over an unconscious body and landed in a puddle of vomit, but when they rounded the corner of the pavilion they could see Wuldric and his lieutenant Tilwald disappearing into the darkness with the smaller boys following them.

Keeping far enough back that they wouldn't be noticed but were still able to keep their quarry in sight, they set out across the home field.

Ordgar had taken on the responsibility of ensuring that there was no outbreak of violence between Wuldric and Engelhard at the wedding feast. Whenever the two halves of the kindred were together there were plenty of opportunities for disagreement and violence, most of them out of his control, but Ordgar knew how important Mæl's wedding was to the kindred, particularly when you thought about the resistance of Æthelwaru's family, so he decided to do what he could to prevent the one possible danger he might be able to control.

Still, Ordgar was not above enjoying any trouble Wuldric might make for himself or reluctant to assist Wuldric in the creation of said trouble, so while Engelhard had spent the evening drinking and formulating one reckless plan after another, Ordgar had spent the evening maintaining a wary surveillance of his older cousin, and patiently explaining the flaws in each plan, successfully aborting a number of bumbling and easily traceable revenge schemes.

However, now that Wuldric had taken himself away from the main celebration, Ordgar sensed a possible opportunity either to catch Wuldric at some mischief of his own or to visit some mischief on his cousin's head that couldn't be traced back to him.

The dogs smelled the boys coming, recognized them from the catalogue of smells in their brains, matched them to their human originators, and understood that they were part of the kindred, but the unusual and rankly provocative smell of monkey piss, like some exotic perfume straight from the sweaty crotch of an homuncular canine nightmare, haunted the smells they recognized like a ghost. The dogs began to get anxious and excited, whining and pacing nervously in the kennel. Several of them barked curious, inquisitive barks that the Dog Man wouldn't have recognized because, monkeys not being native to Elmet, the Dog Man had never overheard his dogs trying to puzzle out exactly what the fock the alien smell of monkey piss *was*.

Wuldric stopped beside the enclosure, attracted by the noise of the agitated dogs, and his little group of followers stopped around him. He stepped close to the kennel and the dogs got a good strong whiff of monkey piss and lunged against the wattle panel, restraint overridden by an instinctive urge to bury their noses in that smell and perhaps tear into it with their strong white teeth. Wuldric twitched backward into Tilwald, who stumbled backward into a smaller cousin everyone just called Flea who had crowded too close behind.

Ordgar and Engelhard faded into the shadows beside the stable to watch.

"The Dog Man will kill them if they fock with the pack," Ordgar whispered. He waited to see if Engelhard would make any connections between the Dog Man, the dogs, and their idiot cousin Wuldric, but the silence stretched out; Engelhard wasn't the sharpest arrowhead in the quiver.

"Too bad he isn't here," Engelhard said finally.

Ordgar could see he was going to have to take the initiative, which was better in the long run because he couldn't trust Engelhard not to fock it up; Engelhard liked to put his personal seal on revenge so its object had no uncertainty about who was behind his misfortune. This revenge scenario required a more delicate and preferably anonymous touch. He looked at the kennel, which was washed in yellow light and squirming shadows from a few nearby fires and some hanging lanterns, and waited until Wuldric and his cousins moved away.

Ordgar realized that a soaking in monkey piss had ruined Wuldric's mood, which had been rescued from boredom by watching the monkey get drunk on mead. Ordgar imagined that his cousin felt the urge for meanness, which is what he always seemed to feel when he was embarrassed or frustrated. He'd be wanting to change his clothes and revenge himself on the monkey. Wuldric's intense focus on revenge would keep him from seeing that Ordgar and Engelhard were about to visit their own on his head.

"Come on," Ordgar said. He moved quickly out of the shadows and hurried across the open space toward the kennel. Engelhard hesitated for a moment before he followed.

The dogs recognized Ordgar, a frequent presence on Old Torhtmund's *tún* and sometime playmate when they were all younger, and wagged their tails. Ordgar lifted the latch on the kennel gate and opened it wide, squatting to block the opening as the dogs pushed their muzzles toward him to say hello.

"Monkey piss," he hissed. "Monkey piss — monkey piss — dogs, dogs, dogs, monkey piss: Wuldric." He used the Dog Man's tone and rhythm when he wanted to mobilize the pack for pursuit and finished the sibilant incantation with a low wide sweep of his arm to point in the direction Wuldric had gone. The dogs boiled out of the kennel so fast they knocked him over, and he rolled aside as they jumped over him, shouldering into one another, jamming in the entrance, and then the wriggling jam breaking up as they ran after his monkey-piss-stinking cousin.

One of the dogs, a bear hound, thick in the chest, throated a low warbling howl that grew louder and climbed the doggie scale into a higher octave, and several of the other dogs took up the howl as they raced after the exotic stench of monkey. Wuldric turned at the sound of the howling dogs and saw a wide low shadow undulating over the ground toward him and realized that the dogs were loose and he was in trouble. He didn't have a big head start, but he made the most of it, hurtling headlong ahead of his cousins through the semidarkness.

His pack of cousins broke for the gate when they saw the dogs surging toward them, and some of the mutts peeled off to follow. The jostling as the pack separated slowed them a little, improving Wuldric's lead. The smallest boy, Flea, leaped into the lower branches of a tree and scrambled out of reach, but the rest of them, Tilwald in the lead by a good few yards, made it to the gate of the *tún* ahead of the pack and legged it for the pavilion.

Wuldric had gained a couple of steps when the dogs were deciding who to follow, understanding that the primary source of the mesmerizing smell wasn't among the group of smaller boys. Not much of a tree climber, Wuldric ran straight for the only thing that he thought might get him beyond the snapping teeth of the dogs — the wall that enclosed the *tún* — five feet high, two feet wide, mud-chinked dry masonry. He leaped for the top of the wall and fell short, striking it with his gut and scrabbling at the stones to keep from falling back into the dogs. One leaped after him and its teeth seized the cloth wrapping around his leg just as he pulled it over the top of the wall.

Wuldric struggled hard to pull his leg up against the dog's weight and when the encumbrance finally dropped away, his momentum unbalanced him and he fell backward, landing in the home field with a heavy thud that drove the breath out of him. The dogs that had followed him piled into the wall and each other in a tangle of snarls and barks and howls, unable to reach him. Two of them tried to leap the wall, scrabbled at the stones with their hind legs, and fell backward into the pack. Then the alpha dog, a cagy boar hound that had worried many a giant tusker to death, but that was now made temporarily insane as its will and judgment were overwhelmed by smell of monkey piss, disengaged from the scrum and coursed along the wall toward the open gate and the rest of the pack followed.

Ordgar and Engelhard struggled to keep up, their nearly incapacitating laughter working against them. They skirted low burning campfires and leapt the angled guy ropes of tents and reaching the *tún* gate a little behind the dogs and the running boys. They stopped: saw the majority of the dogs boiling along the exterior of the *tún* wall, Wuldric scrambling to his feet, the other boys in panicked retreat with a few dogs barking and snapping at their heels, and then Wuldric bringing up the rear, only just ahead of the remainder of the slavering pack. They were all running toward the pavilion where the wedding guests were dancing to the rhythm of the drums and the melody of the flutes and harps.

"Think they'll make it?" Engelhard asked.

"Let's go see." Ordgar started jogging toward the pavilion, struggling to control his laughter and wiping tears from his cheeks.

Dring

I was introducing **Somerild** and Sprot to whomever I knew in the mob of wedding guests. I told myself it would broaden the experience of my fellow Elmetsætan, but in fact I knew that very few of them would benefit from a broader experience that they would never have an opportunity to put to use. They counted themselves far-travelled if they wandered to a hidage in a different hundred, and even then they packed for an overnight trip. Living in Eoforwic, a port city with visitors from Francia, the Baltic, Andalusia, and even Rome, Sprot and Somerild had a broader experience of life when they went to buy a bunch of turnips for the dinner stew than my kinsmen and fellow Elmetsætan would have if they lived a hundred winters. It was amusing to see them putting it together that a brother and sister from Northumbria, aside from speaking a differently-accented dialect of Anglian, were much the same as any brother and sister of their acquaintance.

Whatever attitude Sprot had, possibly expressed with a counterproductive sneer at their reaction, was balanced by Somerhild's charm. She was one of those people who even the most determined arsehole has a hard time disliking. Sprot's sister had helped us with our inquiries in Eoforwic when I was on the *frith stol* in the cathedral, and she had secured an important clue to the mystery of who was murdering people for their coin, and now she was a fancy goods contractor, providing weaving and embroidery to brighten the bedrooms in Rimilda's pleasure house. When I'd met her she was a single mother and amateur sleuth; in the year since she'd become a more self-assured woman of substance. Her two children were off playing with my four children, comprising one of the many small gangs of children that had splintered from the mob that had collected for Whitgar's party trick.

When he'd drunk enough, Whitgar had pulled his bearskin over his head and shuffled onto the dance floor after the tables were removed, and all the smaller children had baited him as he reared up on his knees and swatted at them and growled and chuffed. When he was finally worn out he allowed the mob of giggling children to pull him down and played dead until they lost interest and went away, and then he crawled off to curl up under one of the tables that bordered the dance floor for a restorative nap. Now the young children were running loose and unsupervised, making their own entertainment and mischief, the way children do at a wedding feast while their elders celebrate.

After we finished our turn around the pavilion, during which Sprot had renewed his acquaintance with Creda, Sentwine, and the *geréfas*, we found space on a bench and sat to watch the dancing.

I saw Ingulf walking around, still asking people if they'd seen his wife.

"This is the way it was in Acaster when we were growing up," Somerild said. "Do you remember that wedding feast when we were small?"

Sprot nodded. He was older than his sister, so his memory of whatever feast she referred to must have been better. "I was young Ordgar's age."

Æthelwaru

thelwaru was watching her grandfather dance when she felt an unusual sensation in her crotch as if her womb were shivering, and then it tightened, slowly at first, getting stronger, peaking, and then tapered off, and then she realized her lap and her thighs were wet, and she looked down at the table to see if Mæl had elbowed over a cup of beer in animated conversation. But even as she looked at the tablecloth she knew that her daughter was starting to come, and she smiled, realizing that she'd won her race with bastardy, and that her daughter would be born after her marriage. She shifted forward and took her weight on her elbows, but easing the muscular tension required to sit upright on the chair only seemed to bring on another contraction.

Mæl noticed her shift of position and put

down his cup and leaned over to whisper to her. "Are you unwell, Little Bunny?"

"Your daughter wants to come to the feast," she said.

"Shall I pour myself a cup, or will my son be a while yet?"

"Pour me a cup," she said and clenched her jaw in the wake of the contraction.

Her tone focused Mæl on the matter at hand and he shook his head to try to drive away the buzz from all the drinking. "Little Bunny," he said. "Are you in pain?"

"Only when the cramps come."

"How long have they been coming?"

"They started before I left the *tún* this morning."

"Mother of Christ," Mæl snarled and stood so fast his chair toppled backward. He swept the plates and platters and pitchers to the floor and lifted Æthelwaru out of her seat and onto the cleared tabletop. "Lie down," he said.

Owolma Eris

The monkey drained the cup of mead and clamped his teeth on the rim. After studying the pattern of movement below, he made his way down from the rafters and across the beams to one of the upright supports. There was a table against the post and one of the small barrels of mead rested on its side in a wooden cradle among a cluster of abandoned horn cups. The monkey watched several men place their cups beneath the tap and twist the handle of the spigot. After a few repetitions of this action the monkey was pretty sure he'd grasped the fundamentals of refilling his cup with golden liquid sunshine.

The monkey waited for a lull in the activity around the mead barrel and climbed quietly down to the table and filled his cup. This was the monkey's fourth cup, and the load was heavy in his brain. The monkey watched the garlanded dancers weaving the dance and became aware of the smell of one of the women's fertility as she passed in the circular dance, the smell stronger and then fainter, stronger then fainter, and the monkey closed his eyes and sighed and started to massage his red cock as he sipped the mead, as content as a monkey separated from his natural environment can be, drunk and horny and wanking as he leaned against a barrel of mead waiting to lose the last tenuous command of his muscle tone and slump into oblivion as he had so many nights before.

The boys made it to the pavilion just as the first of the dogs, focused only on the excitement of chasing something that smelled like the unrepentant soul of wildness — wilder than anything she'd ever nosed in the *weald*, clamped her teeth round the calf of the slowest boy and tripped him onto the platform, one step up from the ground. The boy bleated like a culled sheep and skidded across the boards with the brindle bitch attached to his leg and bowled into a group of gossiping women and brought them all screaming to the ground on top of him and the dog.

There were only four dogs in the first group, one chasing each of the boys. The other three boys vanished into the crowd of guests and dancers with the dogs close behind. Wuldric was only three steps behind his cousins and he hurtled into the revelers with nine more dogs an arm's length from his puckered arsehole, snarling and barking and by now sufficiently worked up by the smell of monkey piss to want to savage anything that moved.

The concentrated and undiluted smell of the monkey in the pavilion, stirred up by the energetic movement of the dancers, clinging to the guests sitting at the tables on the edge of the floor and concentrated on the boards where the monkey piss that hadn't soaked into clothing had been trodden into the wood, made the dogs lose their last shreds of decorum (the Dog Man's dogs were usually well-behaved in a crowd) and they started howling and snapping wildly at the phantasmagoric scents in the air, leaping for the rafters from which the ripe smell of monkey cascaded like a waterfall.

The monkey was terrorized into instant action, responding without thought to thousands of years of ancestral conditioning, no different than if he were surprised at a scum-covered savanna waterhole by a leopard (even though it had never seen a leopard and had only a faint memory of the savanna), but, as he gathered his legs under him to leap for the safety of the rafters, a body struck the table and the mead barrel, lightened by half its contents, hopped out of the cradle and landed on the monkey's long tail in a flash of pain, stealing his momentum in the jump so that the beam remained out of reach and he landed on a woman's shoulders. Her scream was unlike anything the monkey had ever heard, even that time in Rome when those peacocks had caught fire in the brothel, and he put a foot on the woman's head to try another jump, but the woman twisted around and swatted at the monkey with both hands, and the monkey lost his tenuous perch on her shoulders and jumped sideways.

Lullo had pulled himself unsteadily to his feet and was trying to make his way outside, away from the panic and the trampling feet, when the monkey landed on his shoulders and wrapped his tail around the *mæsse-thegn*'s neck to keep from falling. Suddenly Lullo was being strangled and he reached up and felt two stone of hysterical monkey clinging to his neck and head. He spun around and his heel hit the edge of the raised hearth in front of the head table, toppling him backward into the fire.

As Lullo fell toward the flames, his arms flailing for balance, the monkey thought of the inferno of the flaming peacocks in the Roman brothel and leaped onto another passing guest, and then he was running across the quaking terrain of the crowd, from shoulder to head to shoulder, as wedding guests converted their rhythmic dancing to spastic writhing in their struggle to avoid the leaping, snapping dogs, and discovered a drunken screaming monkey climbing on them like the penultimate joke in the third act of a lost, lesser play by Aristophanes called, *The Monkey*, a forgotten, third-place winner at the *Dionysia*.

Men were shouting and trying to control the dogs as the boys darted through the crowd, but the dogs had spotted the frantic monkey, clawing and struggling to escape into the rafters, and they were now intoxicated by the frenzied smell of fear-soured-monkey-piss and they lunged, snapping after the terrified simian. The monkey's destabilizing weight pulled men and women off balance and put him closer to the snapping teeth of the equally frantic dogs.

Lullo scrambled out of the fire, his cloak ablaze, remembering what St. Paul had said about marriage, and ran across the dance floor screaming and trailing smoke and flames as he struggled with the clasp of his cloak, remembering, inexplicably, the Latin he had diligently refused to apply himself to in the monastery, yelling, "*Christe adiuva me Uror ego me moriturus.*"

He leaped out of the pavilion, illuminating a section of the home field as he ran, scattering guests who'd stopped to collect themselves in the darkness as soon as they were safely clear of the monkey panic inside. Light and shadow writhed in the darkness as the crowd parted, but one man, less drunk or more sensible, tripped the flaming priest to the ground, threw his own cloak over him, and rolled him in the dewy grass to extinguish the flames. Lullo writhed in pain, shouting a torrent of garbled Latin, as if he'd been struck by a bolt of Pentecostal lightning and could only speak in tongues.

Inside, the monkey was on the floor, weaving among the legs of the wedding guests with the dogs scrabbling after it, and people were jumping away, tripping into one another, and falling in a tangle of shouts and screams and curses. The riotous pounding and screaming finally roused Whitgar, who rolled out from under the table still wearing the bearskin just as the monkey took a hard left turn and found himself running straight at what appeared to be a large bear. With a scream, the monkey leaped onto the bear's back, and from there onto a table, and from there he jumped blindly for the sanctuary of an overhead beam, succeeding finally in getting out of reach.

One of the dogs leaped at the monkey but hit Whitgar instead, knocking him onto his face, the dog snarling and yowling as the smell of musty bear filled his snout. Unfortunately, instead of the security of the empty lattice of joists and beams, the monkey found Wuldric cowering there, daring to congratulate himself on having climbed to safety, and when the monkey landed on his back Wuldric lost his balance and they both plummeted off the beam, the monkey riding him down with rough barks and monkey screams, gripping the back of his tunic with his feet and pummeling Wuldric's ears with both fists.

Wuldric hit the table face first with the

monkey on his back and howling dogs surged over them both. Wuldric rolled to the ground with dogs pulling at his piss-dampened tunic from six directions, and the monkey jumped onto the back of the largest dog, wrapped his tail around its middle, grabbed both its ears, and bit it hard in the scruff. The dog launched itself out of the howling confusion of teeth, and then began spinning around as it tried to dislodge the monkey.

Ðring

I **scrambled onto the table** and pulled Somerild
up after me. Sprot looked around, calmly drain-
ing his cup, and then joined us.

"I told Rud that the monkey would be trouble," he said.

"That's probably why he brought it." I looked
around the pavilion and spotted Rud in the chaos,
clutching a post on the edge of the dance floor,
sagging helpless with laughter.

I put my arm around Somerild and reached up
to grip the beam to steady us as the table shivered
underfoot when a fleeing guest careened into it.
From my position above the heads of the people
still on the floor I had a clear view of the wedding
table, where I saw Mæl shove the pastry model of
his *tún* aside and lift Æthelwaru onto the boards.
She drew up her legs and pointed her knees at the
ceiling as she gripped the sides of the table and
arched her back. I'd seen that spasming position

257

before and I knew what it meant.

"I'm going to be an uncle," I said.

"Let's drink to it," Sprot said, looking around for a pitcher.

The monkey rode a large bucking dog across the empty dance floor with three more dogs snapping behind it, missing the monkey but nipping the flanks of the dog, goading it into even wilder bucking contortions, and then the Dog Man jumped out of the darkness onto the dance floor and looked around and started shouting and kicking dogs as he reasserted his dominance of the pack. The dog with the monkey on his back leaped over the head table and disappeared into the darkness outside, but the monkey dismounted in mid-leap, bounced once on the table, and scrambled up the prodigious wide chest of Æthelwaru's father, Eadnoth, to disappear into the rafters.

Eadnoth tried to pull away when the monkey climbed up the front of his tunic, and the force of the monkey hitting his chest was all it took to overbalanced chair and send him backwards. I saw his booted feet kick at the rafters and then there was a splintering crack as the chair came apart under his weight and a loud thud as he hit the boards.

A boy stumbled to his feet, bleeding and bitten, wailing and disoriented. A small dog hung by its teeth from the bloody hem of his tunic. There was something familiar about the boy, but it took me a moment to recognize him as the boy that my nephew Engelhard had knocked into the mud last year in the market in Loidis. His moustache was only a little less wispy now, but made fuller by the clotting blood from his smashed nose. Then I looked around for Engelhard and spotted him and Ordgar standing at the far edge of the pavilion watching the unfolding havoc with big smiles. I felt a transient emptiness in my gut, and I knew they'd had a hand in what was happening, though I didn't know how. At least they were keeping their distance now and were not involved in the turmoil.

The Dog Man finally reestablished dominance over the dogs and there was a moment's silence in the pavilion. The floor was empty, except for Whitgar standing there like the Lord of Misrule in a bearskin, trying to understand what was happening, possibly wondering if that had been a real monkey or a monkey of the mind, and Æthelwaru's grandfather, who was dancing by himself with his eyes closed and his arms spread away from his sides. There were fifteen or twenty people standing on tables around the pavilion, but most of the rest of the guests had fled into the night. I imagined them shuffling around out there in the dark home field, taking stock, counting their fingers and toes, wondering what the fock had happened as they looked back at the dance floor where the Dog Man was furiously shouting at his dogs, telling them that they'd embarrassed themselves and him and the kindred and they'd all suffer for it.

Two of Derehild's sons-in-law had lifted her chair off the floor and set it onto a table, and the men of her side of the kindred had gathered protectively around her, facing outward in a defensive phalanx. I doubted that she was in any real danger. The Dog Man's mutts were slinking around with their tails tucked in that chastened, guilty posture that dogs assume when they know they've angered their master, although I doubted that they were feeling anything close to guilt. I saw them peering up into the shadows where the monkey had disappeared when they thought the Dog Man wasn't looking. If the monkey had dropped to the floor they would have been all over it in a heartbeat, despite the Dog Man's red-faced shouting.

At the head table there was a gaggle of concerned women around Æthelwaru and they all seemed to be trying to take control of the birthing, but Mæl was resisting their attempts to move him out of the way.

"My son's coming out to see me, and I'll be here to meet him," he shouted, and they backed a little away, except for my mother who was used to Mæl's temper and not cowed by the volume of his complaints.

"How many babies have you delivered?" she demanded.

"How many have you fathered?" her son demanded in turn.

I thought he'd argued her to a draw with that *non sequitur*, but she ignored him and moved close to the table again and took Æthelwaru's hand.

Eadnoth's sons crowded around him and rolled him to one side and spun him around so his legs were over the edge of the floor, extending out of the pavilion, and then they pulled him upright into a sitting position. The top of his head bobbed into view behind Mæl. When he looked over his shoulder, I saw that his face was red and puffy, like a bull's scrotum after a run through a tall patch of nettle. He was shouted something that didn't seem to be language.

Eadnoth's oldest son, Osnoth, said something to Mæl. Mæl ignored him, but Æthelwaru jerked her head around and then reached out and grabbed a fistful of Osnoth's tunic, and, before anyone could prevent her, pulled herself into a sitting position on the table and punched her brother with her free left hand so hard that he fell back backward over their father, who was still sitting on the floor trying to get his bearings after the apparition of the monkey, which would no doubt haunt his sleep for years.

Æthelwaru shrugged aside any attempts to restrain her and hopped to the floor, her left hand now supporting her belly, and took a step toward her nearest brother. She grabbed his hair and drove his head into the tabletop. There were a couple of muffled thuds as his face smashed into the cheese wheel. (Damn, that had been good cheese, too.) Mæl recovered from his surprise and put both arms around her shoulders to restrain her. From the security and stability of his embrace, she put her foot on her father's back and shoved him off the raised platform into the darkness on top of her brother.

With a great shrug, she threw off her husband's arms and went for her next closest brother, who was hemmed in by the press of women who'd clustered around the head table to help with the birthing and couldn't escape.

"You beat my Furry Badger?" she screamed.

"Mæl," Old Torhtmund shouted from the other side of the panicking crowd of women. "Control your wife."

"Ha," my brother snorted. "Have you met Æthelwaru?"

"Christ's beatific ball sweat," I muttered.

"What does she mean?" Somerild asked.

"Her brothers set on Mæl in the woods last spring and beat him shiteless to discourage the courtship," I told her. "He never let on he knew who it was and he didn't retaliate because they're Æthelwaru's brothers. Kept it all secret, except he told me just before I left to work for Offa."

"Well, it's not a secret anymore," Sprot said.

Æthelwaru grabbed the front of her brother's tunic with both hands and drove her forehead into the middle of his face. We could hear his nose break from where we were, and two gouts of blood shot down into his beard as he went weak at the knees. She drew her leg back to kick him in the balls but suddenly grabbed the edge of the table and moaned. Mæl lifted her onto the boards again, then took a pillow from the chair and slipped it under her head.

Another of her brothers came to help the one with the broken k but, he must have invaded Mæl's personal space because my brother swatted him out into the darkness with an absent-minded sweep of his arm, on top of the growing pile of men related to his wife.

Æthelwaru

"**I'm well done with you** after today my girl," my father said. I kept my mouth shut. It seemed that I'd kept my jaws so tightly together for so long that they ached. I'd been done with him for a long time: done with his laziness and gluttony that made him the size of an ox; done with his greed for a bigger bride price because he wanted to use Mæl's desire to marry me to put coin in the chest and add to his hidage; done with his envious complaints that Mæl's kindred was so rich they'd never notice the loss of some silver and land if they really wanted to buy a bride for the great fool; done with his ridiculous pride that insisted our kindred was too ancient and important to make a downward marriage with Mæl; done with his delaying the wedding in the hope that grandfather would die and leave him as head of the kindred so he could call it off; done with his pathetic lust for the milking girls that he thought no one knew about; and done with having a father like some great sinner collecting all seven of the deadliest, and snow wouldn't melt in his mouth while he told me what to do and not do, the way he'd done all my life.

Waves of pain and memory, rising and falling, swelling and receding, one overwhelming the other and then being absorbed into it again. This must be what grandfather feels like. I'm afraid for him. and I cry out as the pain replaces a memory of this morning, when I climb onto the waggon, holding my belly in my hands, and lower myself onto the chair in the waggon bed. The linen curtains that hang from the frame that encloses the chair move in the slight breeze and the long garlands of ivy and holly and the trailing ribbons swing. My mother and sisters climb into the second waggon. My brother Osnoth drives the waggon. If he drives recklessly the baby will come before the wedding. I see my father giving Mæl his bastard when we get there, laughing and telling him he's appealed for spoiling his virgin daughter.

"Æthelwaru."

I open my eyes. It's night, and the stars float over my head, and I'm on my back on something hard. Men walk beside me. I recognize the *geréfas*. It must be Northumbria. I'm wounded in the slaughter at the *tún,* and now they're carrying me back to the horses. I can't ride, but they didn't leave me. I feel stabbing pain and reach for the wound, but instead of blood there's a great belly and something moves inside it. Who is that screaming? It sounds like the woman who beat Mæl's nephew. She can't take her eyes off the *seax* as it hisses toward her neck.

"Æthelwaru."

There's a woman walking beside me. How did Mæl's mother get to Northumbria? I'm cold. My clothes are sweat-soaked.

"The baby's coming," she says.

Something moves inside me, and I know it's a monkey, covered in dun-colored fur.

"If you appeal him for rape," you'll never be head of the kindred. Your brother Eadmer was always a better son. And you were in your mother's belly when we married. Live with it."

Grandfather rages. Mostly he's quiet, and sometimes he's afraid, but when he rages I feel like my father must feel. Was he my father? Was my father his father?

"Mæl's better to me than you were my whole life," I say.

He slaps me. "You're a whore," he shouts.

My grandfather looks far away into another time and says nothing.

I hit my father back. "If you think I'll get old and wipe your fat arse when you're too weak and sickly to do it, you're wrong." I say.

"I'll beat the bastard out of you," my father shouts.

"Go ahead," I shout. "Mæl will kill you, and I'll laugh."

y sister, **Beomona,** puts the flowered wreath on my head and stands back to look, and then leaves me alone. I stand in a linen dress stretched over my belly, a linen veil held in place by a wreath, and soft leather shoes tight on my feet, thinking, *not yet my girl, not until the priest Jaruman says you're married, so your daughter's not a bastard.*

The first cramp comes so slow it seems I watch it come from a long way off, and I have time to prepare, the way you prepare for any hard work, getting my mind right and my muscles ready. It's irresistible as floodwater—rising up, cresting, and receding. I breathe through it and feel it go leave and brace myself, but nothing happens, and I wait and breath and wait, and then I go outside and get on the waggon.

Grandfather Wulfnoth sits on his horse in his good cloak with the woven hem and the embroidered design, and he waves at me, and I wave back, and we start for Old Torhtmund's *tún*.

Little Bunny," he says.
　　I open my eyes and Mæl looks down at me. He holds my hand. I must be dying.
"Don't bury me in Northumbria," I say.
"We're in Elmet," he says.
"I don't remember the ride," I say.

Horses aren't as slow as oxen. The waggon sways from side to side as wheels find ruts, and I hold onto the arms of the chair until my fingers ache, and I pass through one, two, three more slow cramps that started far away and take their time. They twist my guts. They radiate from the center of me—fill me up and drain me. I concentrate on the farthest thing I can see, a tree, a hill, a bird in the sky, floating in the distance. I close my eyes and breath slow.

My brother Osnoth stops the waggon and my grandfather rides ahead to the *tún* while my father says, "You're a willful bitch and pregnant to boot, and I'm well rid of you. No good's going to come of this," he said. "Mark my words, you'll kill him or he'll kill you, and the only question is: how long will it take?"

"How much longer?" I say.

Mæl's mother looks between my legs and says, "A while yet."

Mæl's sister wipes my face with a damp cloth. The *geréfas* stand nearby. The hall is warm and bright from the blazing hearth fire. Mæl holds my hand.

"How did you get to Northumbria?" I asked Mæl's mother.

"You're in Elmet, Little Bunny" Mæl says.

"Don't little Bunny me," I say. "Shut it tight and keep it shut."

Mæl's father hands him a cup.

"I'm gutted, and you're having a drink?"

"You're having a baby," Mæl's mother said. "It only feels like you're gutted."

I hold out my hand and Mæl takes it. Another pain starts to build, and I feel it in my ears and toes, and my thighs are warm and wet.

"Am I bleeding?" Gut wounds bleed.

Mæl leans over me and whispers, "No blood, Little Bunny. You just pissed yourself."

The priest Jaruman is standing beside Mæl. "Are you here to give me the last rights?"

"I'll pray with you if you want," he says.

"Pray for that bitch that beat Mæl's nephew," I say.

"I pray for all of them," he says. "Every night."

"Then get out of here, and let me do what I have to do," I tell him.

At least I'm married, I think. *At least my girl*

269

won't be a bastard.

"**W**ake up, Little Bunny," *a voice says.* *"Wake up. Try to drink something."*
And I open my eyes, and I'm still in the hall, and Mæl's mother and sisters are there, but no one else besides Mæl, still holding my hand. Mæl's sister Enflæda is washing me with a warm, wet cloth, and his other sister Eadgiþ is holding a cup of cold water to my lips. It tastes so good. There's mint in it. I sip and close my eyes, and she tilts the cup until I shake my head, and she takes it away.

"How long have I been here?"

"Two or three hours," Mæl says.

"How much longer?"

Mæl's mother puts her hand on my belly and looks between my legs again and says, "The baby's in position, and you're getting ready."

I'm happy I'd resisted the birth until we were married. I feel weak and drowsy, and I leaned back and take deep slow breaths. I can feel sweat on my neck and on my face.

I think about the wedding. I go through it in my mind, so I won't think about the pain. We exchanged blades — Mæl gave me his *lang-seax* and I gave him a *lang-seax* my grandfather wanted him to have to protect the family. Then the ritual sods — the *handgeld* and *brydgifu* — Mæl's brother and my brother exchanged squares of fresh-cut thatch.

And then Mæl's brother handed two gold rings to Jaruman.

I put my arms around Mæl and kissed him, and he held me with his big arms around me and our daughter, and we felt safe.

And I stood beside Mæl as another pain came on, still slow then, but building faster than the others had, and I heard the Latin and smelled the candles, and the chapel all faded away, and I relaxed against Mæl, and he supported me as the cramp became everything in the world and held on longer than the others and then drained away again.

I remembered the cold of the sweat on my face and taking deep breaths and standing up straight. I reckoned then it had been three hours since that first cramp, and I knew babies come in their own time, and it might be over in hours or it might take a day, and I knew that there was hard work coming, but I knew what hard work was, and I'd seen babies born, and I just wanted to get through the feast and then lie down with Mæl and birth our daughter.

I didn't know anything.

It was good to see the men I'd gone with into Northumbria—the *geréfas*, and Hring's and his Frisian friends, and the Northumbrian *geréfa*, and Ordgar and Jaruman, and even Mæl's father's Master of Hounds, the Dog Man. We'd all shared a thing no one else would ever share, and worked a work that needed doing, and come back a family in blood and respect.

I felt my gut contract uncontrollably and felt the baby move, and I was lightheaded and weak-legged and wrung out by the pain, like I was in a machine that was all agony and gears with mismatched teeth. I'd look for their faces and remember fighting beside them and riding back from Catræth, and I knew that if I was strong enough to do that, and if they accepted me for who I am, then having a baby wouldn't kill me, and I was glad they were there to see my daughter come into the world.

And then my water broke and feasting was over.

Mæl lifted me off the floor, and I was on my back again, and there was a pillow under my head, and Mæl's mother Flæd was bending beside me whispering into my ear, "breathe, breathe," and wiping my brother's blood off my face with her sleeve.

"You'll be all right, Little Bunny," Mæl kept saying over and over.

Another contraction wiped everything else from my head except the pain at the center of the world and the feeling that a calf with stone hooves was trying to climb out of my womb, and I knew that whatever was down there was too big to come out.

And even though I'd struggled to keep her in, now I had to push her out; there was no other ur-

gency in the world but to push harder than I'd ever pushed to expel her, and I thought of how the
mares and cows and sows and ewes and dogs I'd
seen give birth had never seemed this distressed
by it, had never appeared agonized by the act of
delivering their young into the world. Then the
pain had gone, and I was floating on the surface of
a calm lake of warm water, and a sort of stillness
came over me and that sense of wellbeing I drifted
in after sex with Mæl, and then there was a smell
I'd never smelled before, a smell that was me and
not me, a new smell that drew me toward it, and
then there was a baby crying, loud and nearby.

"It's a daughter," I heard Flæd say.

Something thick and ropy flopped against my
thigh with a warm sticky wetness, and I felt it
slide along, and then there was a weight on my
chest as Flæd laid the baby between my breasts. I
knew that the smell was the smell of the baby, and
I inhaled her and closed my eyes as Flæd placed
my hand on her back. She was still connected to
me by the ropy cord. Under my palm, I could feel
the waxy film that covers babies just out of the
womb, like bits of crumbling cheese, moist and
warm.

"Wait," Mæl's sister Enflæda said. "There's
another one."

And when she said that, as if her words caused
it, I felt another urgency to push, intense and irresistible, and I spread my knees wider yet and bore
down, and then again, keeping the baby on my

breast steady with my right hand and gripping the edge of the bed with my left, and arching my back, breathing in that smell.

Then there was another floating, drifting, head-blurring release and another smell, different than the first smell but somehow the same. I knew it was the smell of Mæl and me blended together into two new people, and then Flæd said, "This one's a son."

And I felt another warm wet rope on my other thigh and Flæd guided my hand left to my breast as I felt a second weight beside the first, and smelled the second smell, and the smells were the same but different, and different from all the other smells in the world. The moist fenny smell of my insides and blood and nakedness — musty and sweet like the smell of damp sheets after sex — the smell of the lives we'd made.

"There's two, Little Bunny," Mæl said, and he kissed my forehead. I opened my eyes and looked at his upside-down face, grinning and crying. "A son and a daughter, and they're all red and covered in blood and some kind of waxy, whey-looking shite, and they're angry."

I looked down and saw the tops of two small heads with fine wet hair and little clumps of the pasty white shite that Mæl was talking about.

"Which is which?"

"This is our son," Mæl touched the one at my left breast. "And this is our daughter."

They wriggled when he touched them.

Enflæda leaned over me and draped a soft woolen cloth over the babies. An unbelievable feeling of peace came over me, because I had my babies and they weren't bastards, and I was so happy. I remembered beating my brothers and kicking my father out of the pavilion, and I felt even happier, and I realized that I was smiling a smile so wide it made my face ache, and that I was crying at the same time. I felt that if I could beat up my brothers and then pass two babies the size of small ponies through my cunny, there was nothing I couldn't do, but at the same time I felt so comfortable with the babies on my breasts that I never wanted to move.

"Mæl," I said.

Mæl's head loomed over me.

"Why did you never tell me my brothers beat you?"

"Would've just caused trouble," he said. "You're worth a beating."

Then I loved him more than I'd ever loved him. We stayed like that for a time, and I knew that people were moving around in the long house. I heard the *geréfas* shouting that I'd had two babies and calling for mead and beer so they could drink toasts. Someone built up the hearth fire to warm the big room, and the babies were calm, their naked skin against my naked skin, and then I felt something big and wet and warm ooze between my thighs. I made a surprised sound because I thought there was another baby.

"Shussshhhh," Flæd said. "It's just the after-birth."

Flæd lifted the afterbirth up to show me. It looked like a raw calf's liver. I saw that the two cords were both rooted in it. Flæd set it aside and tied off the cords with her bloody hands and took her scissors from her belt and cut them. The babies stirred on my breasts and moved their heads, but they were sleepy and didn't try to suckle.

Mæl leaned over and whispered, "It's almost sunup. It's time for the morning gift."

"I know what the morning gift is," I said.

"I've another," he said, and held a small wooden chest where I could see it, and then he opened it and spilled out a gold chain that had two large amber pendants attached. They were the deep reddish yellow of honey, and I could see small bubbles trapped in them. He reached into the chest and took out two amber earrings.

"And I've a morning gift for you," I smiled. "A daughter and a son."

I must have gone to sleep then, holding Mæl's hand.

Ðring

I **climbed down from the table** and turned to help Somerild. Sprot stayed where he was, looking around at the ruins of the wedding feast. At least a dozen tables had been knocked off their trestle bases, and a barrel of beer had been overturned. A couple of the dogs had sidled away from the Dog Man's tirade and were lapping up what hadn't drained through the cracks in the boards.

The *geréfas* were moving around the head table. Flæd was giving orders and pointing. Enflæda picked up the two cloaks that my girls had woven and used them to cover Æthelwaru.

"Ready lads?" Rædnoth asked. "Lift."

Four of the *geréfas* lifted that section of the table off the trestles and stepped away and two more stepped up front and back, and they carried Æthelwaru out of the pavilion.

"Enflæda, Eadgiþ, run ahead to the house and get the bed ready."

My two sisters ran out of the pavilion and disappeared into the dark as the *geréfas* followed, keeping the table section level, and Mæl kept pace with them, holding Æthelwaru's hand and telling her that she'd be all right.

Sprot jumped down and walked off with some definite purpose in mind, and Somerild and I sat down on the bench and took a breath. It seemed like I hadn't taken a breath since the dogs charged in. I looked at Somerild and laughed.

"Is this what that wedding feast was like in Acaster?"

"I remember more dancing and not as many monkeys," she said.

"I reckon my brother's going to be a husband and father on the same day. He was always a bit impatient."

Sprot came back carrying a pitcher and some cups.

"All I could find was cider," he said. "But it's tasty."

He sat the cups on the table and poured.

"I saw you sort the *tún-geréfa* earlier," I told him. "I'm obliged."

Sprot shrugged dismissively. "Your sister deserves better than a wanker taking liberties."

"He'll be looking for another job tomorrow," I said.

"He's looking for another job now. I was dead clear on that point."

Out on the floor, old Wulfnoth was dancing in a slow circle with his eyes closed and from the darkness outside I heard the advocate Ingulf calling out, "Thryth, where are you? Has anyone seen my wife, Thryth?"

Whitgar was standing with the bearskin over his head and shoulders, and when he saw us, he shuffled slowly in our direction. Sprot reached to a nearby table and picked up an overturned cup and snapped a little bit of liquid into the air. By the time Whitgar got to us, Sprot had filled it from the pitcher and it was waiting on the boards to be drunk.

"I'm going to go up to the hall to see how Æthelwaru's doing," Somerild said, and touched my arm as she walked away.

Sprot watched his sister step into the darkness and had a sip of cider. "I think she might be sweet on you."

"I doubt it." I hadn't seen Sprot's sister in a year, and the little time I'd known her had been concerned with the business of finding a killer. And now, even if I were interested, she was in Eoforwic and I was heading south in a week, back into Mercia to meet Banta in Tamoworthig.

Whitgar stopped in front of us. He was wearing the bear's head like a hood, the long snout ending in the black nose, yellow fangs pointing down like icicles. I handed him the cup of cider and he drained it in long slow swallows, tilting his head until the bear's head flopped back between his shoulder blades. He lowered the cup and burped with the contentment of a man who knows the purgative benefits of a good burp.

He looked around the nearly deserted pavilion, littered with abandoned cups and spilled pitchers, the whimpers of the terrified monkey drifted down from under the thatching above our heads. I reckoned that as much as people would be waking up sweating from dreaming about the monkey, the monkey would be doing the same.

Derehild's sons-in-law were lifting her down from the table, still enthroned in the carved chair. Æthelwaru's brothers were dazed and bleeding at the head table. The Dog Man was driving the last of the yelping dogs out of the pavilion in a blue cloud of curses and intricate profanity that linked their disappointing and reprehensible behavior to wolves and Mercians. The patriarch of Æthelwaru's kindred was dancing by himself beside the smoking, scattered remains of the fire in the hearth that Lullo had fallen into, and we could hear Lullo moaning out in the darkness, a mishmash of self-pitying Latin and Anglian and some private dialect of his personal confusion, still attempting to rediscover the speech of men. Up in the house, Æthelwaru was screaming Mæl's name.

Whitgar gestured for Sprot to refill his cup, and pronounced his benediction on the outcome of the day.

"Jesus Christ at Cana, this might be the best wedding I've ever been to."

If you have enjoyed this book, please go to its Amazon book page and leave a short review. It will be most appreciated!

OTHER BOOKS BY THIS AUTHOR:

The Deepest Sea
[ISBN: 978-1-940469-24-9]

Bran Snorrison, aspiring *skaald* in the Norse town of Clontarf, becomes entangled in a situation involving the sister of his friend and lord and the son of the local Irish chieftain. Caught between his duty and his growing attraction to a woman beyond his station and financial resources, he goes on his first *vik* to make the brideprice in plunder from the Mercians, and to eliminate his rival, if the opportunity presents itself. Unfortunately for Bran, the Norns have something else in mind.

The Frith Seat
[ISBN: 978-1-940469-22-5

It's the spring of 783, and people are being murdered in Eoforwic. That doesn't mean much to Hring, recently an assistant advocate in Elmet, and currently a drunk, grieving the loss of his wife. When he's falsely accused of murder, he seeks refuge in the frith seat in the cathedral, where he has 40 days to make his peace with God—who he's not sure he believes in anymore—before facing his unjust punishment. For Hring, it's 40 days he can use to hunt down the real killer.

The Peace Weaver
[ISBN: 978-1-940469-23-2]

The Peace Weaver is a collection of stories set in the latter years of the 8th century. The first story, "*Friðo-webba*," centers on an assignment to escort a young woman who has volunteered to become a peace weaver between two feuding kindreds to her wedding and her new home. The second story, "The Bean Spoon," involves the investigation of an apparent suicide. The Third story, "Village Geometry," takes place when Hring is accompanying the commissioners who are taking the census for the Tribal Hidage for Offa of Mercia. The final Story, "The Swift Flight of a Sparrow," picks up Hring's life 12 years after the events of "Village Geometry," when he is working as a spy in Northumbria.

The Elf-Shot Boy
[ISBN: 978-1-940469-20-1]

The Elf-Shot Boy is a story about a boy named Ælfgar (Gar) who has what we now call Down syndrome. Just before the midsummer assembly, when boys Gar's age become legal adults, symbolized by getting an iron weapon, a girl called Oshild is raped and murdered. Everyone thinks Gar is too simple to become a legal adult, but he takes it upon himself to help Hring, the assistant advocate in town for the assembly, investigate the crime. They discover that Oshild apparently stole the only copy of a charter that proves ownership of a nearby estate, which is being contested at the midsummer *gemót*. The more they investigate, the stronger the connection between the murder and the theft becomes. This promises to cause trouble for everyone, but all Gar is concerned about is avenging Oshild's murder and getting his iron.

Beweddian
[ISBN: 978-1-940469-21-8]

You can pick your friends, but you can't pick your family; as far as your family goes, you just have to make the best of it. Hring's misanthropic brother Mæl, who operates a grist mill for the kindred, unmarried at the advanced age of 34, has fallen in love with the equally difficult daughter of a neighboring kindred, and no one is in favor of the match. They've picked each other, and they're resolved not to let anything stand in the way: not the objections of their families, not the disharmony between different branches of Mæl's kindred, not even a wedding gift with an agenda of its own.

BOOK CLUB DISCUSSION QUESTIONS

1. How did the voices and tones of the narrators affect how you experienced this book? I a more modern voice a help or a hindrance?

2. Describe the main characters — their personality traits, motivations, inner qualities. Did any of the characters remind you of people you know?

3. Was the plot engaging — did the story interest you?

4. What main ideas — themes — does the author explore?

5. What passages struck you as insightful,

6. Was the ending satisfying? If so, why? If not, why not?

7. Did this novel change your understanding of the historical period?

8. What was the author trying to accomplish (entertain the reader, deliver a message?)

9. Would you read another novel by this author? Why?

ABOUT THE AUTHOR

Charles Barnitz is an accomplished author who has published stories in *The Denver Quarterly* and *The Madison Review* and had a chapter of his novel, *Mummers*, anthologized in the *Signet Classic Book of Contemporary American Short Stories*. His cult favorite, *The Deepest Sea*, will be released in a new edition this year from Blood And Thunder Press. Many of his stories follow Hring, an 8th-c. former monk, now serving as an assistant advocate in the gemót courts of the Mercian province of Elmet. He is out to see balance restored, even if it takes a little creative interpretation of the law to bring the guilty men to the rope.

Visit Charles at his website at:

www.charlesbarnitz.com

www.ingramcontent.com/pod-product-compliance
Lightning Source LLC
Chambersburg PA
CBHW021949170626
46808CB00001B/78